EXTRAORDINARY

ASIAN AMERICANS
and
PACIFIC ISLANDERS

SUSAN SINNOTT

EXTRAORDINARY
ASIAN AMERICANS
and
PACIFIC ISLANDERS

REVISED EDITION

Children's Press®
A Division of Scholastic Inc.
New York • Toronto • London • Auckland • Sydney
Mexico City • New Delhi • Hong Kong
Danbury, Connecticut

SAN DIEGO SCPA

Interior design by Elizabeth Helmetsie

Library of Congress Cataloging-in-Publication Data

Sinnott, Susan.
    Extraordinary Asian Americans and Pacific Islanders/Susan Sinnott—Rev. Ed.
      p. cm. — (Extraordinary people)
    Rev ed of: Extraordinary Asian Pacific Americans. 1993.
    Includes bibliographical references and index.
    ISBN 0-516-22655-X (lib. bdg.) 0-516-29355-9 (pbk.)
    1. Asian Americans—Biography—Juvenile literature. 2. Pacific Islander Americans—Biography—
Juvenile literature. [1. Asian Americans. 2. Pacific Islander Americans.] I. Sinnott, Susan.
    Extraordinary Asian Pacific Americans. II. Title. III. Series.

    E184.O6 S558 2003
    920'.009295—dc21   2002011220

To Nathaniel and Lucy, extraordinary by any measure

Contents

50

D.T. Suzuki
1870–1966
Philosopher, Teacher

61

Pablo Manlapit
1891–1969
Filipino Labor Leader

74

Philip Vera Cruz
1904–1994
Labor Leader

53

Mary Kawena Pukui
1895–1986
Author, Translator,
Editor

64

James Wong Howe
1899–1976
Cinematographer

77

Anna May Wong
1905–1961
Actress

55

Chiura Obata
1888–1975
Painter

67

Dalip Singh Saund
1899–1973
Member, U.S. House
of Representatives

80

S.I. Hayakawa
1906–1992
U.S. Senator, Scholar,
College President

58

**"Sessue" Kintaro
Hayakawa**
1890–1973
Film Star

70

Isamu Noguchi
1904–1988
Sculptor

83

Hiram Leong Fong
1906–
U.S. Senator

86

Toshio Mori
1910–1980
Writer

89

**Bienvenido
N. Santos**
1911–1996
Writer

92

Carlos Bulosan
1911–1956
Writer

97

Ahn Chang-Ho
1878–1938
Social Activist

97

Philip Ahn
1905–1978
Film and
Television Actor

101

Chien-Shiung Wu
1912–1997
Nuclear Physicist

104

Minoru Yamasaki
1912–1986
Architect

106

**Spark Masayuki
Matsunaga**
1916–1990
U.S. Senator

108

I.M. Pei
1917–
Architect

111

Joyce Chen
1918–1994
Chef, Restaurateur,
Businesswoman

114

An Wang
1920–1990
Computer Wizard

118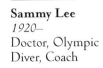

Sammy Lee
1920–
Doctor, Olympic
Diver, Coach

121

Yoshiko Uchida
1921–1992
Children's Author

130

Chen Ning Yang
1922–
Winner, Nobel
Prize for Physics

142

Toshiko Akiyoshi
1929–
Jazz Pianist, Composer,
Band Leader

124

Jade Snow Wong
1922–
Author, Ceramicist

133

Patsy Takemoto Mink
1927–2002
Member, U.S. House
of Representatives

145

Chang-Lin Tien
1935–
University
Chancellor

127

Daniel K. Inouye
1924–
U.S. Senator

136

K.W. Lee
1928–
Investigative
Reporter

149

Norman Mineta
1932–
U.S. Congressman,
Secretary of Commerce,
Secretary of Transportation

130

Tsung Dao Lee
1926–
Winner, Nobel
Prize for Physics

139

Gerald Tsai Jr.
1928–
Financier

152

Nam June Paik
1932–
Video Artist, Composer

155

Yoko Ono
1933–
Artist, Musician

166

Bette Bao Lord
1938–
Writer

179

**Internment
Camp Inmates**
1942–1945

159

Seiji Ozawa
1935–
Conductor

169

**Maxine Hong
Kingston**
1940–
Writer

186

**Gordon Hirabayashi,
Fred Korematsu,
and Minoru Yasui**
Internment
Resistance Fighters

162

Zubin Mehta
1936–
Conductor

172

Bruce Lee
1940–1973
Martial Artist,
Actor

191

Ellison S. Onizuka
1946–1986
Astronaut,
Aerospace Engineer

164

Allen Say
1937–
Artist, Illustrator,
Photographer

175

Dith Pran
1942–
Journalist

194

Connie Chung
1946–
News Anchor,
Reporter

197

Lawrence Yep
1948–
Writer

207

Gary Locke
1950–
Governor

217

Elaine Chao
1953–
Secretary of Labor

199

June Kuramoto
1948–
Musician

209

Eugene H. Trinh
1950–
Physicist, Astronaut

220

Ang Lee
1954–
Film Director

202

Wayne Wang
1949–
Film Director

211

Amy Tan
1952–
Novelist

223

Yo-Yo Ma
1955–
Cellist

204

Vera Wang
1949–
Fashion Designer

214

Myung-Whun Chung
1953–
Musician, Music
Director, Conductor

226

Gish Jen
1955–
Writer

229

David Henry Hwang
1957–
Playwright

241

Midori
1971–
Violinist

255

Hmong Refugees
1970s

232

Maya Ying Lin
1959–
Architect, Sculptor

244

Kristi Yamaguchi
1971–
Figure Skater

259

Tiger Woods
1975–
Golfer

235

Greg Louganis
1960–
Olympic Diver

247

Michael Chang
1972–
Tennis Player

262

Michelle Kwan
1980–
Figure Skater

238

Jerry Yang
1968–
Internet Entrepreneur

250

**Vietnamese
Boat People**
1970s

266

Anoushka Shankar
1982–
Sitar Player

Introduction

In my introduction to the first edition of this book, *Extraordinary Asian Pacific Americans*, I compared the wide range of biographies with the images on a piece of Chinese silk. The subjects may differ widely one from another, I explained, but they all had an "artful canvas" in common. Now, ten years later, it does not seem necessary to apologize for linking people of such different backgrounds. Today "Asian Americans and Pacific Islanders" makes for a familiar canvas.

Yet "Asian American" is still a relatively new concept. Before the late 1960s, white Americans considered immigrants from China, Japan, Korea, or the Philippines together as "Orientals." Among themselves, Asian and Pacific Island immigrants identified more with their countries of origin. These nations often had long histories of conflict and violence with their neighbors, making it hard for those from such countries as Korea and Japan, for example, to celebrate a common identity on this continent. Similarly the Chinese who had escaped the murderous regime of Mao Zedong in the late 1940s considered themselves anti-Communists above all else. They eyed

Asian American student activists of the 1960s and 1970s suspiciously, since they believed they were soft on communism.

Time, however, has a way of changing one's perspective. Most of this book's new biographies are of men and women who never lived in Asia. Their parents may have escaped political turmoil in their native lands, but when they settled in America, they vowed to leave their troubles back home in order to turn the American dream into reality for their own children. Through a disciplined work ethic and tremendous sacrifice they made sure their sons and daughters studied at some of America's finest colleges and universities. And, following their parents' examples of diligent effort, these men and women have risen to the tops of their fields. Yet these successful Americans have not lost sight of what makes them different.

As I researched this book, one phrase seemed to summarize these records of achievement. *A Clear Strong Vision* is the title of a documentary film about the life and work of Maya Lin, the brilliant architect and sculptor who designed the Vietnam Veterans Memorial in Washington, D.C. These words seem to describe not only Maya Lin's life and work but also that of many of her fellow Asians and Pacific Islanders. It also speaks to the source of their success: A clear strong vision brought Maya's parents here from China after Mao Zedong seized power and allowed them to imagine a future of limitless opportunity. It sustained them in the hard work of making a life here. This, in turn, led to their daughter's confident ability to express her own creativity.

The contributions of the latest crop of extraordinary Asian Americans has made me wonder what this book will be in another ten years. With Tiger Woods, Vera Wang, Ang Lee, Amy Tan, Jerry Yang, Yo-Yo Ma—to name just a few—setting the standards of excellence in their fields, will another book even be necessary? Very soon, it seems likely, the adjective "extraordinary" will describe these Americans very well on its own.

Davida Malo

Author, Translator
1795–1853

Long before the arrival of Captain Cook in 1778, and the European traders and American missionaries who followed him, the cultural life of the Hawaiian Islands was rich and active. The native Hawaiians lived in gentle harmony with all that nature had given them. That we know anything about the lives and customs of these remarkable people is due to the work of Davida Malo and, especially, his book *Ka Moolelo Hawaii: Hawaiian Antiquities.*

Davida Malo was born in 1795 in Keauhou, the area of North Kona on the island of Hawaii. Both his parents were members of the court of King Kamehameha I, where he spent most of his childhood. While in the courts of the high chief Kuakini, Davida Malo learned about the traditional life and lore of the Hawaiian chief society. During this time he also met American missionaries in the courts and received his first Christian instruction.

Malo's parents encouraged their son's inquisitiveness and supported his eagerness to learn. While still in his teens he married the daughter of the king of Maui. His new wife, A'alaioa, was much older than Davida, but it was customary for bright young men to increase their status by marrying royalty. A'alaioa died only a few years after their marriage, and Davida Malo then moved to Lahaina, Maui.

At Lahaina, Malo met the Reverend William Richards, a Christian missionary. He studied English and religion with the minister and in 1828 was baptized. During this time Malo and Reverend Richards worked on a translation of the Bible, which would later have a deep impact on religious life in Hawaii. Malo also began keeping a record of Hawaiian genealogies, or accounts of family histories from earliest times.

Malo was able to begin his formal education at the newly opened Lahainaluna Seminary (high school) when he was thirty-eight years old. As one of Hawaii's first native-born Christians, he strove to be a good example to his fellow students. He worried that the other seminarians weren't nearly devout enough and spent too much time drinking and fighting at "trading places," as he once wrote.

Malo's first literary work, a religious tract, was published in 1831 and eventually sold thousands of copies. His other writings warned the islands' chiefs to improve communication among themselves or risk losing everything—including their uniquely Hawaiian way of life. "The ships of the foreigners have come and smart people have arrived from the large nations. . . . [T]hey will eat us up, such has always been the case with large nations, the small ones have been gobbled up."[1]

Malo's views were controversial in Hawaii, but his presence was hard to ignore. He became a successful businessman, growing sugarcane and producing molasses. In 1841 he was appointed general school agent for the island of Maui. He was later named superintendent of schools for the kingdom and then was elected representative from Maui to Hawaii's first house of representatives.

After the death of his second wife, Batesepa Pahia Malo, in 1845, Davida fell in love and married a beautiful young woman named Lepeka (Rebecca). Although this marriage caused Davida considerable grief, Lepeka gave him his only child, a daughter whom he named A'alaioa after his first wife.

By 1850 Malo was so distraught by both his marital problems and his sense that Hawaiians were losing the islands to foreign traders that his health began to fail. Shortly after becoming an ordained minister, he took to his bed and refused to eat or drink. He died at Lahaina, Maui, in 1853.

Malo finished the first volume of *Hawaiian Antiquities* around 1840, but the entire work was not translated into English until 1903, fifty years after his death. With its publication, the full breadth of Malo's intellect and influence was finally realized.

Yung Wing

Educator, Diplomat
1828–1912

Yung Wing spent his life straddling two very different cultures. One foot was placed in the country of his birth and ancestry, China; the other was firmly fixed in his adopted homeland, the United States. He felt close to both yet a part of neither.

Yung Wing was born in the village of Nam Ping near what was then the Portuguese trading colony of Macao. Because Macao was a bustling port, with clipper ships arriving often from all over the world, Yung Wing—unlike many other Chinese of his day—was familiar with the West. His parents, influenced by the bustling local shipping trade, decided their son's success in life depended on his obtaining a Western-style education.

Their wish was granted when, with the financial help of a minister in China from Yale University, three Chinese boys, including Yung, were selected to attend a preparatory school in the United States. In April 1847 Yung Wing arrived in Massachusetts and enrolled at Monson Academy. He adjusted well to his new life and new school and, after graduating in 1850, wanted nothing more than to be able to stay in the United States. There were two problems, however. First he had promised his parents he would return to China after two years, which he had already extended to three. Second was the matter of the high cost of continuing his studies.

Two sponsors came forth to fund Yung's education and after many pleading letters, his parents agreed that it was in their son's best interest to stay in America. In 1850 Yung Wing became both a Yale freshman and the first Chinese ever to enroll at an American college.

Yung Wing rose to the academic challenges of Yale. "I never was subject to such excitement," he wrote one of his sponsors those first few months. "I enjoy its influence very much."[2]

He also threw himself into Yale's extracurricular activities, sometimes literally. Shortly after arriving on campus, Yung became something of a football hero. Each year the entire freshmen and sophomore classes competed in a football free-for-all, where everyone rushed onto the field and the first team to score a touchdown won. Yung Wing, dressed in old clothes and with his long queue, or pigtail, tucked underneath a cap, took to the field but stood nervously near the sideline. When the ball landed at his feet, however, he grabbed it and began to run as fast as he could.

At first everyone thought he had taken the ball back to the sideline, but then someone spotted him heading toward a nearby street. The other players, more than 200 of his fellow students, hurried after the fleeing figure. As one spectator described it, Yung "bounded like a deer; he flew on the wings of the wind. His hat went off, his queue burst from the pins and streamed behind him like a pump handle. The whole college ran after him with yells of anger and delight."[3]

During his years at Yale, Yung Wing developed an affinity for the West. He appreciated its way of life and thinking. In 1853 he became a naturalized U.S. citizen. Still, when he graduated, he was confused about the direction his life should take and for various reasons decided to return to China.

Back home Yung tried to convince the imperial government of the great importance of sending Chinese boys to school in the United States. He firmly believed that for China to be able to enter the modern world, her people would need technological training available only in the West. Yung himself looked forward to the day he could lead a Chinese educational mission in the United States.

After working several years as a silk and tea importer, Yung Wing was assigned by the imperial Chinese government to a post in Washington, D.C. China needed a trade negotiator and Yung Wing was the most qualified person in China to do business with the Americans.

Before leaving for Washington, Yung Wing again proposed the idea of an educational mission to the government in Beijing. To his surprise, the response was favorable. Even normally close-minded government officials were beginning to see the value of instructing young men in the uses of Western technology. In 1872 thirty Chinese boys were sent to Hartford, Connecticut, to study, with thirty new students to follow each year of the program.

In 1875 Yung Wing married a white American, Mary Kellogg. With his marriage, the ties that bound him to China became increasingly loose. His links to his adopted homeland, on the other hand, seemed unbreakable.

At the same time, China set up its first permanent mission in the United States and named Yung Wing associate minister, that is, second in command after the ambassador. His fluent English made him popular with

U.S. officials, and he used his influence to improve the lot of Chinese workers in the United States. He was outraged by the prejudicial treatment they received and he didn't hesitate to say so.

Despite Yung's sincere efforts, the Chinese education mission lasted fewer than ten years. Officials of China's imperial government worried that Yung Wing was less interested in training Chinese youth in Western technology than in encouraging them in Western ways of life.

In 1881 he was summarily called back to China to take stock of his government duties. He stayed one year, returning to the United States as soon as he heard of his wife's grave illness. Mary Wing died in 1886, and for the next ten years Yung lived quietly in Connecticut raising his two sons, writing, and lecturing.

In 1898, just short of fifty years after becoming a naturalized American, Yung Wing was shocked to receive a telegram from the U.S. State Department telling him his citizenship had been revoked. The reason given was that a change in the naturalization law had made his earlier application invalid. Yung begged friends to help him, but no amount of influence changed the government's mind.

Yung left the United States and settled for a while in Hong Kong. However, in 1902 Yung managed to return to this country, slipping in undetected by immigration authorities. He lived out his life in Hartford, near his sons and their families. He was visited by American and Chinese friends and consulted often on questions of U.S.–China relations. In 1909 his autobiography, *My Life in China and America,* was published. It was the first English language memoir written by an Asian American.

Queen Lydia Liliuokalani

Hawaii's Last Monarch
1838–1917

In the 1890s, Americans—or "mainlanders," as the Hawaiians called them—were eager to take charge of the remote Pacific Islands of Hawaii. American government officials were clear in their belief that, however charming the monarchy might be, the queen needed to understand that she could reign but not rule.

Queen Liliuokalani, however, saw things differently. Descended from the prominent chiefs of the "Big Island" of Hawaii and sister of King David Kalakua, whose death in 1891 brought her to power, she believed only native Hawaiians must rule their islands. King Kalakua had struggled to hold off the influence of the haoles, or Caucasians, but he had been a weak leader.

When Liliuokalani took the throne, she was determined to prevent the Americans from gaining any more strength. She knew that American sugar planters wanted to annex Hawaii in order to ensure a firm market for their product.

After assuming power in 1891, Queen Liliuokalani made sweeping changes in all branches of the government. In January 1892 she threw out the old cabinet and then, in a stunningly theatrical move, proclaimed a new constitution. The new document restored many of the royal powers her brother had bargained away. When, at the last moment, two legislators refused to sign, the queen's anger matched her ambition. As Liliuokalani stormed about her royal residence, those who opposed her new constitution gained support.

Several American businessmen moved quickly to turn legislators against the queen. Within a year a small group of Americans and Europeans, aided by the United States Marines, took over the Hawaiian government. Sanford B. Dole, a Honolulu-born American lawyer and plantation owner, was made governor of the Provisional Government of Hawaii. Unable to stop the overthrow of her kingdom, Queen Liliuokalani was placed under house arrest.

A counterrevolution in 1895 led to Liliuokalani's brief imprisonment, and then, in 1898, Hawaii was formally annexed by the United States. The former queen retired to her lovely residence, Washington Place, wrote an angry book, *Hawaii's Story by Hawaii's Queen,* and returned to her first love, music.

All the members of Liliuokalani's family were musically gifted but Lydia was the most gifted of them all. At four she was able to sight-read music and had perfect pitch. Tutored privately, she developed a deep understanding of Western music and was able to blend its melodies with Hawaiian instruments. She performed often at the royal palace, playing the piano, ukulele, guitar, zither, and organ with great skill.

"To compose was as natural for me as to breathe," she once wrote. Indeed, one early piece, "Aloha Oe" ("Farewell to Thee"), written in 1878, was the first Hawaiian song to become popular outside the islands. She also wrote a Hawaiian national anthem, "He Mele Lahui Hawaii," in 1866, although another anthem was adopted in 1876.

Although Hawaii's political problems may have caused Lydia Liliuokalani great bitterness and distress during her lifetime, the sounds of Hawaii's lovely music lifted her spirits. Her contribution to its preservation gave her life meaning and enriched the world.

Travelers to Gold Mountain

1848

In the villages of Canton Province, news of the comings and goings of trading ships at the nearby port of Hong Kong was eagerly awaited. As soon as a clipper docked, crowds gathered to hear the tales of its well-traveled crew. The lands across the sea, it seemed, were full of wondrous treasures. When, in 1848, word spread that gold had been discovered in faraway California, the lure of *Gum Shan*—the Mountain of Gold—was too strong to ignore.

To be sure, the risks of leaving China were great. In emigration, as in other matters, the policies of China's imperial government were harsh. Young men were needed for the emperor's army and for public works projects, and so any men caught leaving their homes and families to work abroad would certainly face the executioner's axe.

And, as if the death penalty were not enough, the would-be emigrant also had to go against the teachings of Confucius that guided the Chinese in all matters of daily life. Confucius taught that children must devote themselves to their parents and ancestors. Leaving one's family and ancestral home, therefore, was a grave offense against Chinese tradition.

What then would make a young Chinese man risk everything to sail for the Mountain of Gold? Simply that he had everything to gain—even life itself. Canton is a rocky, barren province, and at the time, its farmers could grow only enough food to feed the large population for four months out of the year. Because there was no industry, the only way for the Cantonese to assure their own survival was for every family to send at least one male abroad.

As stories spread up and down the coast—from Hong Kong to Macao—that the streets of this fabulous place called California were paved with gold, families prepared their young men for the hard journey. The first of the Gum Shan Hok (the guests of Gold Mountain) were not disappointed. And neither were their families back in Canton. Packages of gold dust and nuggets arrived from California, and before long the province became the most prosperous in China. Streets were paved and lit, schools were built, and well-stocked markets were opened for business.

Not surprisingly then, more and more men sought passage to America. Even after California's generous gold vein gave out, thousands clamored for the opportunity to work across the ocean. The rewards were so great that families did everything possible to get one of their own onto a ship. By 1851, 25,000 Chinese "guests" were in California.

What were the experiences of these thousands of young men? In her book *Mountain of Gold*, Betty Lee Sung tells the story of a young Chinese named Fatt Hing Chin, whose story is typical of other early emigrants to the United States.

As nineteen-year-old Fatt Hing tried to earn a living peddling fish at the wharves of Kwaghai, he heard stories of the Mountain of Gold. News of this faraway place had become almost as valuable to local people as the goods bought and sold on the docks. Soon Fatt Hing made up his mind to seek his fortune on the distant mountain. He knew of the dangers. Many, he had heard, had been arrested boarding ships and taken off to certain death. But he had heard, too, that certain soldiers could be bribed, and he took the time to find out which ones. Then, with great difficulty, he convinced his worried

Chinese miners on the Mountain of Gold

parents to sell a water buffalo and some family jewelry in order to pay the high price of smuggling himself onto a Spanish ship bound for San Francisco.

The passage took three months. The ship's hold was full of other young men who, like Fatt Hing, were illegal stowaways. For the first time in Fatt Hing's life, he was surrounded by strangers. Many became sick during the long voyage and some died. All were miserable. By the time the hills of San Francisco came into view, many of the Chinese wondered if, in fact, they would live long enough to see any gold at all.

When the ship finally docked though, the stowaways were relieved to see several Chinese men waiting for them on land. These men greeted the new arrivals and took them to the headquarters of the Six Companies, or the Chinese benevolent associations, in San Francisco's Chinatown. There the men were fed and given tea and told a bit about what to expect in America and at the gold mines.

"One valuable lesson we have learned and which you will soon appreciate," the chairman of the Six Companies told Fatt Hing and the others, "is that we must stick together and help one another, even though we are not kin. That is why we have formed this organization called the Six Companies, representing the six districts which most of us come from."[4]

The chairman continued by telling the arrivals how to get along with the white miners, who were often rude and rough and would try to provoke the Chinese. "Be patient and maintain your dignity," he told them. The Six Companies supplied the new workers with mining tools and advised them where and how to start. Within days of arriving in California, the men headed for the hills, where they were relieved once again to see camps filled with fellow Chinese.

The new miners worked furiously to loosen the earth from the mountainsides and wash out the fine gold particles. Unlike other miners, who had the advantage of working new claims, the Chinese were assigned only leftover claims. Still, Fatt Hing was very happy with his small portion of gold dust, which he quickly sent back to his family in China. He did not tell them about the ill treatment and humiliating prejudice he faced every day. Once he scribbled a single message inside one of his packets: "Truly these are mountains of gold!"

When profits in gold mining began to decrease in the mid-1860s, Chinese laborers started leaving the gold fields for jobs in railroad construction and fieldwork and for limited employment opportunities in San Francisco. Prejudice and discrimination, however, followed close behind.

Polly Bemis (Lalu Nathoy)

Idaho Pioneer
1853–1933

Nineteen-year-old Lalu Nathoy waited in the San Francisco customs shed for her turn to stand before the immigration officer. She thought of the long journey she had just completed from China in the hold of a cargo ship and of the terrible suffering and sorrow she had witnessed. She tried not to let loneliness, fear, and home-sickness overwhelm her.

Lalu Nathoy (later called Polly Bemis) was born in China in 1853, a period of famine and political unrest. Her parents struggled desperately just to harvest enough food to survive and to pay for the upkeep of their tiny farm. To help support the family, Lalu's parents considered hiring her out to wealthy landowners as other families had done with their daughters. But Lalu Nathoy pleaded with her father to allow her to stay at home and work beside him in the fields.

Before Lalu could work in the fields, however, she had to have her tightly bound feet unwrapped. In China it was customary to wrap little girls' feet with cloth so they would remain small and delicate. Unbinding her feet and letting her work like a man would bring shame and insults and jeopardize her chances for marriage. Nevertheless it was what she wanted. And so for the next five years, Lalu Nathoy worked beside her father in the fields. Yet the famine throughout the region continued, and with the desperate conditions came marauding bandits, who swept into villages on horseback and carried off anything of value.

One day bandits rode up to the Nathoy's home. There was no food or livestock for them to take, but one man seized Lalu and threatened to kill the entire family if she did not go off with him. Her father had no choice but to accept the two bags of soybeans offered as payment. Lalu Nathoy never saw or heard from her family after that terrible day. Eventually she was sold to a Shanghai brothel owner, who, in turn, offered her to a "special buyer" in America.

When the San Francisco immigration officer finally finished questioning Lalu, she was taken to a Chinatown marketplace. There she was auctioned to the highest bidder and put on a ship that sailed up the coast to Portland, Oregon. From there a Chinese man drove her along many miles of rugged trail to the makeshift mining town of Warrens, Idaho. In Warrens, Lalu Nathoy was delivered to her new master, a Chinese saloon owner named Hong King. And it was there that she began answering to a new name, Polly.

Polly's old, miserly owner cheated and abused her. After a while she devised plans for running away and even thought about how she could get rid of him. Freedom came to her, however, in an unexpected way. One day Hong King lost everything he owned in a poker game to a fellow Warrens saloon owner named Charlie Bemis, and King had to forfeit his right to ownership of Polly. For Polly, this meant that her luck had finally turned around.

Charlie Bemis gave Polly two things she had not known for a long time: freedom and love. With these gifts and the money that she was now able to save, Polly opened a fourcroom boarding house in Warrens, where she became one of its most trusted and respected citizens.

Townspeople talked often of Polly's rare ability to make others happy and healthy. Once, when Charlie had been shot in the head by a drunken customer and the local doctor gave him no chance of recovering, she nursed him back to health by applying Chinese herbal medicines.

Polly ran her popular boarding house until she married Charlie in her late forties. The two then headed into the Idaho wilderness, where they homesteaded twenty acres of land along the Salmon River. After Charlie died in 1922, Polly Bemis lived in their rustic mountain cabin for as long as she was able to manage on her own. When she died in Warrens in 1933, the entire town turned out to honor her.

Unfortunately, Polly Bemis's story is one of the very few with a happy ending. Such luck never caught up with most of the young women who were kidnapped in China and then sold into prostitution. For many, passage to America was truly a death sentence.

Chinese Laundry Workers

1850s

The neon sign of a Chinese hand laundry reminded Charles of the several shirts he had not yet picked up. . . . He entered the shop and saw the old man still hard at work behind the counter, ironing under a naked electric bulb, although it was already ten o'clock at night. . . .

"How many years have you been in the States?" Charles asked out of curiosity as he paid the man.

"Forty years," the old man answered in Cantonese. No expression showed on his face.

"Do you have a family?"

"Big family. A woman, many sons and grandsons. All back home in Tangshan." From underneath the counter he brought out a photograph and showed it to Charles. In the center sat a white-haired old woman, surrounded by some fifteen or twenty men, women, and children of various ages. The whole

Chinese laundries, like this one, opened even in small, isolated towns during the late ninteenth and early twentieth centuries.

clan, with contented expressions on their faces, were the off-spring of this emaciated old man, who supported not only himself but all of them by his two shaking, bony hands.[5]

By the late nineteenth century the passage of anti-Chinese laws had already forced many Chinese workers out of most agricultural and manufacturing jobs. Competing with whites had become both difficult and humiliating, so the Chinese, in large numbers, began opening laundries. With just a washtub and an ironing board, one could open a business and earn a modest living.

By 1886, 7,500 Chinese were engaged in the laundry business. Despite the fact that laundries were not common in China and most Chinese men considered washing "women's work," male Chinese immigrants in the United States learned how to make the laundry business work for them. Laundries allowed the Chinese to be their own bosses and to work within the Chinese community, thereby avoiding daily discrimination. Knowing how to speak English well was not a requirement for opening a store. Most launderers never needed to know more than a few English words to run a successful business.

As the Chinese left the large cities of California and headed East, they found that they could open laundries almost anywhere. In large cities such as Denver, St. Louis, and Chicago, they could find low-rent quarters, put out a sign, and begin taking in laundry almost immediately, while living in the same place. Because they provided pickup and delivery, the location and appearance of the store was unimportant. Many other Chinese laundries were located in white neighborhoods where Chinese usually were not allowed to live. So launderers lived instead in the overcrowded ghettos of Chinatowns.

It's not surprising then that for at least half a century, the main occupation of the Chinese in the United States was washing and ironing. In 1920 there were four Chinese laundries for every Chinese restaurant, the other common business.

The money sent to China by laundrymen often allowed large extended families to live comfortably. Usually a family relied on a single person working long, lonely hours in the United States. Many never knew the hardships a Chinese worker had to endure in America. Laundry work was boring and lonely. The income provided for only a modest standard of living. Because many immigrants had gone into debt to pay for their passage to America, a good deal of their income went toward the repayment of their loans. A little was taken out for living expenses, and the rest was sent to their families in China who depended on it for their survival.

In time many new arrivals saw laundry work as more of a prison sentence than a job. They worked day in and day out but dreamed only of the day they could return to China. In the words of one young man interviewed about fifty years ago:

> People think I am a happy person. I am not. I worry very much. First, I don't like this kind of life. . . . To be a laundry-man is to be just a slave. I work because I have to. . . . After you are at it for so many years, you have no more feeling but to stay on with it.[6]

Most of those who entered the laundry business stayed with it until far into the twentieth century. Today, new Chinese (along with other Asian) immigrants are opening dry cleaning stores, shoe repair stores, and other quick cash-flow businesses that require a minimum of English and allow the whole family to work.

Chinese Railroad Workers

1860s

Years of bickering preceded the decision in 1862 to build a transcontinental railroad in the United States. With the Civil War threatening to pull the nation apart, Congress quickly passed the Pacific Railway Act, which was then signed into law by President Abraham Lincoln. The law gave financial backing to two companies—the Central Pacific and the Union Pacific—to lay the track that would link the East Coast to the West Coast.

Among the problems encountered by the Big Four railroad tycoons—Charles Crocker, Leland Stanford, Collis P. Huntington, and Mark Hopkins—was where to find workers for such a huge project. Charles Crocker, who was head of construction for the Central Pacific, decided to try Chinese labor. He had heard that, despite being physically small, the Chinese worked hard and long for very low wages. Crocker believed that they, unlike the Union Pacific's mostly Irish crews, would not risk striking to gain better wages or working conditions.

Chinese workers take supplies to railroad crews as a Central Pacific supervisor looks on.

With this in mind, Crocker recruited fifty Chinese workers and sent them, picks in hand, to the Central Pacific work site. From the first day they performed beyond anyone's expectations, working without complaint for fourteen hours. Impressed by their conduct, Crocker immediately began recruiting Chinese laborers from Chinatown and later directly from China. By 1869 nearly 15,000 Chinese workers were employed by the Central Pacific. Competition was fierce between the Union Pacific, which was working its way west through Nebraska and Wyoming, and the Central Pacific, which was making its way eastward through the Sierra Nevada. Because the U.S. government was paying the companies for the miles of track laid, construction bosses pushed their workers hard.

There was never any question who had the more difficult task. The Central Pacific had to pick its way by hand through the huge granite walls of the Sierra Nevada that rose steeply to heights of 7,000 feet (2,134 meters). The Union Pacific crews, on the other hand, made their way through the more gradual rise of the Black Hills. Many wondered if any humans could complete the task facing the Central Pacific's Chinese workers—first the steep mountain faces, then the bitter cold, the blinding snows, and the avalanches during one of the coldest winters in western history. At one point during the winter of 1865–1866, almost 5,000 men were put to work just clearing snow. They dug tunnels beneath the huge drifts and for months traveled like moles from living quarters to work, scarcely seeing above the snow's surface.

As the heroic work of the Chinese became known, the Irish workers of the Union Pacific began to openly express their jealousy. The leaders of each railroad used this spirited competition to get even more work from their men. Once when the Central Pacific laid down 6 miles (9.7 kilometers) of track, word was quickly sent to the Union Pacific bosses. The next day, the proud Irish answered back with 7 miles (11.3 km). Near the finish point,

Charles Crocker wagered $10,000 that his Chinese workers could lay 10 miles (16.1 km) of track in one day. Thomas Durant, president of the Union Pacific, accepted the bet. The Chinese completed the 10 miles and added 56 feet for good measure!

These Chinese pioneers, who laid 689 miles (1,109 km) of railroad track, contributed greatly to opening up the West to commerce and settlement. Yet, when the last spike—the Golden Spike—was driven into the railroad ties on May 10, 1869, at Promontory, Utah, linking the Central Pacific and Union Pacific railroads, no Asian workers were included in the historic photograph. This omission foretold worse things ahead as 25,000 railroad workers poured back into California looking for new jobs.

By 1870 unemployment in California was dangerously high. Political leaders, eager to find a scapegoat for the state's economic problems, blamed the hardworking Chinese. And the Chinese, who stood out in their traditional dress and long queues, or pigtails, were easy targets. Shortly after being praised for their extraordinary work on the railroad, the Chinese were openly scorned and even attacked by disgruntled workers. As the nineteenth century came to a close, the Chinese of California found themselves in an even more uncertain situation than when they had first arrived to work on the railroad.

Sugarcane Workers in Hawaii

1870s

I n 1877 the *Hawaiian Gazette* proclaimed, "Sugar is . . . King!" and everyone on the islands agreed. Sugar production had become Hawaii's main industry, thanks largely to the flow of eager workers from China, Japan, Korea, and the Philippines. And the plantation owners knew that if sugar's reign was to be a long one, they would need even more workers in the future. So, beginning in the 1890s, the call went out to all able-bodied Asians to come work on the islands. By 1920, 300,000 had signed on and were settled at one or another of the huge Hawaiian sugar plantations.

At first Hawaii seemed like a dreamland to the new arrivals. The climate was close to perfect, the soil was rich, and the green mountains seemed to hang from the clouds. Once settled in a sugar plantation, however, the realities of life became much different. All of a sudden, the family unit—of greatest importance to Asians—had to take second place to the rule of the

A feared luna, or foreman, watches closely to make sure sugar cane stalks are properly bundled.

plantation owner and his *luna,* or foreman, who were usually whites of Portuguese descent.

It was no longer the sun that announced each new day for these workers but the shrill plantation siren. The lunas and the police strode through the camps making sure all were ready for work. One Korean woman remembered the time her family did not hear the work whistle and overslept. The luna flung open the doors and burst into the room screaming and cursing for everyone to get up and get to work. If someone did not move, he simply ripped off that person's bedcovers.

In the fields laborers wore *bangos,* small brass discs with identification numbers that hung around their necks. No one seemed to care about their names; numbers were used by everyone except one's fellow countrymen.

On the sugar plantations working conditions were extremely bad. The owners treated the Asians like children, threatening them if they misbehaved. They were supposed to be orderly, clean, and prompt and could expect to be fined or even whipped if they disobeyed the long list of regulations.

Still, unlike in China or Korea, there was always plenty of work for everyone. When the cane was ripe, lines of men were led out to the fields to harvest the crop. They worked very fast, swinging their machetes through the forest of 12-foot (3.6 m) high sugarcane.

When all the cane was cut, the workers tied the stalks into bundles and loaded them onto train cars. The train would then pull the cane to the mill. Inside the mill, machines crushed the cane and boiled its juices into molasses and sugar. The loud whir of the machines and the heat from the huge vats left workers confused and exhausted.

The sugar owners tried hard to keep their workers from organizing and staging protests and strikes. By 1900, however, many Asian workers could no longer ignore the poor working conditions and low pay. Many had learned to read and knew of the higher wages paid for farmwork on the mainland. They talked of these things among themselves and began to question their labor contracts and even to plan strikes.

Soon tension between workers and owners increased. In 1903 one luna hit a worker and was immediately set upon by a gang of Chinese men. In 1904, 200 Korean laborers rioted when a plantation doctor kicked a patient in the stomach. In 1906 and 1909 Japanese laborers went on strike, demanding higher wages and equal pay for equal work.

After years of labor unrest on the sugar plantations, conditions began to improve. As worker organizations and Filipino labor unions gradually developed, plantation owners were forced to change their cruel ways. Then, too, second-generation Asians, who were educated in Hawaii's schools, would simply not work under the same conditions as had their parents. They demanded a different life.

Slowly Asian workers began to feel there was a place for them in Hawaii. They planted gardens and turned work camps into homes. They built their own churches and temples and were allowed to worship as they pleased. They freely practiced their native customs and traditions without suffering the prejudice and isolation that was common in California and the rest of the United States mainland.

In time, these hardworking Asian immigrants became proud of their adopted homeland. Through their suffering and struggle they had transformed these beautiful islands into a society of rich diversity. Many old people could finally say with honest pride, "Lucky come Hawaii!"

Prisoners of Angel Island

B y 1900 stories reaching China of the abundant riches in California were more fable than fact. Anti-Asian feelings among whites in America had made life very difficult for the Chinese. The Chinese Exclusion Act of 1882, which had singled out one ethnic group for discrimination, was never challenged. In fact by the turn of the century amendments to the law made it even harsher than originally intended.

The Exclusion Act attempted to stop all Chinese laborers or their families from entering the United States. The only immigrants welcome from China were officials, teachers, some students, and tourists. This left Chinese workers in America, almost all men, in a desperate situation. Their families in China depended on the money that was sent to them from America. Without income from abroad, many would starve because southern China could not support its large population. But enforcement of the

Women with their children wait to be interrogated at the Angel Island immigration station.

Exclusion Act meant that there was no hope families could reunite in the States.

Many of the young men who had left their homes for America shortly after marrying expected their separation would be brief. Believing this, many wives happily saw their husbands off. As one popular Chinese rhyme suggested:

> If you have a daughter,
> marry her quickly
> to a traveler to Gold Mountain.
> For when he gets off the boat,
> he will bring hundreds
> of pieces of silver.[7]

Indeed, sometimes the silver did arrive and occasionally the husbands returned. In America, however, Chinatowns became full of homeless, lonely men, and in China "widows" raised fatherless children. The strong ties that traditionally bound Chinese families were being broken.

Some Chinese men, desperate to be reunited with their families, looked for any possible loophole in the immigration law. Some tried to convince authorities that they were not common laborers at all but merchants. Others produced papers claiming they were native born. Few of these schemes succeeded.

Help finally came to Chinese laborers in an unexpected form. On April 18, 1906, as Chinatown residents recalled, the earth dragon split the ground beneath the city of San Francisco. Buildings toppled and burst into flames. Nearly 28,000 structures were destroyed by a great earthquake—including the city's municipal buildings, where records of births, deaths, and marriages were stored. Now all of a sudden, there was no way to verify the most basic facts of someone's life.

Many residents of Chinatown took advantage of this opportunity to claim they had been born in San Francisco, and according to U.S. law, their children, even if they were born in a foreign country, were automatically U.S. citizens. As proof of citizenship, the residents forged their own birth certificates and sent money to their families to come to America.

Soon, however, immigration authorities caught on to this tactic and devised ways to make entry difficult. They used the law, which required immigrants to undergo a period of detainment at either Ellis Island in New York or Angel Island in San Francisco Bay, to interrogate Chinese families and force many of them to return to China. Of all Chinese who were detained at Angel Island, 10 percent were sent back to China.

All immigrants coming through Angel Island had to pass an examination to prove their American identity. They were not released until they had convinced authorities that their identity papers were legitimate. Often the questioning, which was designed to confuse and trick immigrants, went on for hours. Usually it had nothing to do with whether the person had a right to enter the United States or not. For example, someone might be asked small details about his or her life in China: "How many chickens did your grandfather own? Where was the village pond? What did your mother's water jug look like?" Answers were checked against those of relatives and any differences were taken as proof of fraud.

San Francisco's Angel Island was known for its unsanitary conditions and unfair interrogation procedures. The building where immigrants were originally detained was a two-story shed that extended out over the water, connected to the wharf by a narrow stairway. The small, smelly rooms were bare and resembled cages in a zoo. Minimal amounts of food were served—usually thrown—on the floor. Some Chinese waited in these squalid conditions for up to four months before authorities called them in for questioning.

Ironically, because of the interrogations, many who had the legal right to enter the United States were often denied it. They simply were not aware that they would be asked pointless, rambling questions and, as a result, could not adequately prepare. In time, the immigration law and the way immigrants were processed through Angel Island became so twisted that authorities could not tell who should and should not enter the country. It was not until 1943 that the Chinese Exclusion Act was repealed.

D.T. Suzuki

Philosopher, Teacher
1870–1966

During most of the last twenty years of his life, D.T. Suzuki lived in New York City. He could have lived in Japan, where he was considered a national treasure. But New York was a youthful place, he felt, and he loved its energy. Many Americans knew and admired this scholarly man, who had spent his long life explaining the mysteries of Eastern religion to the West, and they allowed him great freedom.

Daisetz Teitaro Suzuki was born into a family of physicians in 1870 in Kanazawa, Japan. It was assumed that he, too, would enter medical practice, but the untimely death of his father made the cost of a full-time university education impossible. Instead, young Daisetz Suzuki spent much of his time at a nearby Zen monastery, studying Buddhism with an honored teacher.

It was his Zen master and teacher who introduced Suzuki to the publishing world in the United States. On his teacher's recommendation, the young twenty-seven-year-old was hired as a translator by Open Court, a small publishing company in LaSalle, Illinois. He moved there and collaborated with Dr. Paul Carus, a noted scholar of oriental philosophy. Together they translated from Chinese several books, which were published in the early 1900s.

These books, including the works of Tao Te Ching and a volume called *Awakening of Faith in the Mahayana*, helped Westerners grasp the differences between their religions and those of the East. Zen, for example, is a branch of Buddhism that was developed in China around A.D. 600 and later brought to Japan, where it had a profound influence on the culture. Zen (from the Japanese *zazen*, meaning "to sit and meditate") strives to free the mind of useless clutter. Through quiet reflection the practitioner of Zen seeks enlightenment—in other words, the ability to understand what is true and meaningful in the world.

D.T. Suzuki left Illinois in 1908 and traveled to Europe. There he lectured at various universities and became famous for his role both as interpreter of Eastern religious ideas for the West and Western religious ideas for the East. In 1909 he returned to Tokyo to teach English at the Imperial University. Later he moved to Kyoto and taught at Otani University where he was a professor of both English and Buddhist philosophy.

Professor Suzuki's opposition to the Japanese military buildup before and during World War II caused him to spend most of the early 1940s under house arrest. He continued writing, however, and his books, such as *Introduction to Zen Buddhism* and *Essays in Zen Buddhism*, became classics in the field of comparative religion.

In 1951 Suzuki moved to New York City, where he lived until just before his death in 1966. During that time he held posts of visiting professor

at Columbia University and the University of Mexico. Until well into his nineties, he amazed his younger friends and colleagues by flying around the world to lecture at universities such as Oxford, Cambridge, and Munich as well as Stanford, Chicago, and Harvard.

D.T. Suzuki became a living example of the doctrine he preached. He seemed, to even casual acquaintances, to have thought through life's large questions and reached a peaceful certainty that radiated from within.

Mary Kawena Pukui

Author, Translator, Editor
1895–1986

Nature lavished her gifts on the Hawaiian Islands, and the native Hawaiians composed songs, chants, and poems to sing of her splendid beauty and to celebrate her long history and heroic rulers and gods. That these songs have survived and are today available in written form, in both Hawaiian and English, is due to the efforts of Mary Kawena Pukui, fondly called "Hawaii's greatest treasure."

Born on the Big Island of Hawaii in 1895, Mary Pukui was of Hawaiian, Samoan, and English ancestry. Her early interest in Hawaiian mythology led her to become a *Kuma hula* (hula master). Hula in Hawaiian is more than just a dance; it is a means of communicating, through both dancing and chanting, the adventures and glories of the past. According to legend, hula artists must prove their mastery of chanting at Ka-ulu-a Pao, Kauai, where they stand at the edge of the sea and chant a *mele* (song), so that it can be heard above the pounding waves and forceful winds.

Later Mary Pukui immersed herself in the works of Hawaii's great nineteenth-century poets. Concerned that the ever-growing American influences in her country might diminish its literary traditions, she dedicated herself to translating and preserving them. Mary Kawena Pukui began working with Laura Green, a missionary's daughter who was also committed to preserving ancient Hawaiian texts. Together they worked on several volumes that were published during the 1920s. These included *Hawaiian Stories and Wise Sayings: Folk Tales from Hawaii* and *Legends of Kawaelo*.

Mary was the sole author of *Hawaiian Folk Tales* (1933) and the senior author of the *Hawaiian Dictionary and Place Names of Hawaii* (1957). Her most important work is perhaps *The Echo of Our Song: Chants and Poems of the Hawaiians*, which she wrote with Alfons K. Korn in 1973.

Mary Kawena Pukui lived a long life, which she made richer by her studies and writings. In many ways, as she described to the author Edward Joesting, she never forgot the words she chanted at the edge of Ka-ulu-a Pao when still just a girl:

> Laka dwells in beautiful forest,
> Standing alone at Moohelaia,
> An ohia tree standing up Mauna Loa,
> Love to you, O Kaulana-ula.
> Here is the voice, a gentle voice,
> A gentle chant of affection to you, O, Laka,
> Laka, inspire us.

Chiura Obata

Painter
1888–1975

My aim is to create a bowl full of joy
clear as the sky
pure as falling cherry petals
Without worry, without doubt;
Then comes full energy, endless power
and the road to art.[8]

When Chiura Obata was eighteen and about to be drafted into the Japanese army, he left his homeland for California. He arrived in San Francisco in 1906, intending to stay only a short time before heading for Europe where he would study painting. A side trip to Yosemite and the High Sierra in California, however, so fired his artistic imagination that he decided to postpone his trip east.

Chiura Obata began studying art at the University of California, Berkeley. After receiving his degree, he began teaching at the university.

From 1931 to 1957 he was a professor of art. His long tenure was interrupted only when he, like other Japanese Americans on the West Coast, was sent to a government detention camp following the Japanese bombing of Pearl Harbor in Hawaii in 1941.

Although neither the FBI nor military intelligence at the time officially considered the Japanese American population a threat to national security, the U.S. government began relocating all people of Japanese ancestry who were living on the West Coast to makeshift camps on remote, unused federal lands.

Chiura Obata joined other first- and second-generation Japanese Americans first at Tanforan and then at Topaz, Utah—one of ten detention camps designed to house the Japanese for the duration of World War II.

Chiura Obata believed strongly that he and his fellow artists in the detention camps should continue their work, no matter how bad the conditions. He organized art schools for both adults and children and used his connections at the University of California to have materials shipped to the camp in Topaz. Since no cameras were allowed in camp, Obata hoped that paintings would provide a permanent record of camp life that could be passed on to future generations. The results are stunningly beautiful depictions of this tragic desert exile.

Although Obata was instrumental in inspiring many during his stay at Topaz, his political views angered some fellow Japanese internees. He was considered pro-American in his views. One night, following a political disagreement with another inmate, Obata was hit over the head with an iron pipe. He was rushed to a hospital in Salt Lake City and from there moved to St. Louis, a location that was considered a "safe risk" by the U.S. government. Obata and his family remained in St. Louis until after the war, when they returned to Berkeley.

In *Beyond Words,* a book of drawings and writings depicting life in the

Japanese American concentration camps, Chiura Obata is remembered as one who looked for the best in the dismal surroundings and encouraged others not to despair. As his wife Haruko wrote,

> It [Topaz] was a totally different environment from what we were used to in Berkeley—dry and hot. There were scorpions, too. We never had seen those before. The sunsets were beautiful though. Everybody was always complaining but Chiura would say, "Just look around. . . . We will survive if we forget the sands at our feet and look to the mountains for inspiration.[9]

"Sessue" Kintaro Hayakawa

Film Star
1890–1973

At the height of his acting career, Sessue Hayakawa had dined with two American presidents and was the proud owner of a mansion in Hollywood and a gold-plated Pierce-Arrow car. That, however, was during the silent movie era, when Hayakawa's handsome face and box-office appeal made him much in demand by film producers across the country. However, when the talkie era began, Sessue Hayakawa lost his appeal. By the 1930s his career in Hollywood was all but over.

An acting career was the last thing Kintaro Hayakawa's parents would have wanted for their son. ("Sessue" was the name the young actor used in Hollywood.) The Hayakawas were aristocrats in Japan's Chiba Province with family roots that could be traced as far back as 2,000 years. Mr. Hayakawa, who once was a provincial governor, brought up his sons according to the strict warrior code of the samurai.

Even Kintaro Hayakawa's plans did not include acting. As a teenager, he wanted to become a naval officer. He entered the Navy Preparatory School in Tokyo, from which he graduated four years later. Following graduation, he was accepted by the Naval Academy in Etajima. That summer, however, he ruptured an eardrum while diving and was disqualified from entering the academy. Totally humiliated by this unfortunate turn of events, Hayakawa attempted suicide.

He recovered from the self-inflicted stab wounds, however, and a year later traveled to the United States, where he enrolled at the University of Chicago. Kintaro Hayakawa graduated in 1913 with a degree in political science and planned to return to Japan and enter public life. On his way home, however, he stopped in Los Angeles, where he attended a play staged by a small Japanese theater company. That one event changed his life forever.

Kintaro Hayakawa went backstage after the performance and complained to the director that the performance was weak. He suggested that he could do much better. The director considered his bold offer and after some negotiation turned the company over to the brash young man. In 1914 Hayakawa's talented direction of the play *Typhoon* caught the attention of a Hollywood producer, who decided to make it into a motion picture starring the director himself.

Hayakawa's silent movie career took off. From 1915 through the 1920s he was one of the most popular and highest-paid actors in Hollywood. He and his wife, Japanese actress Tsuru Aoki, socialized with many movie greats—Mary Pickford, Douglas Fairbanks, and Cecil B. DeMille. When the silent movies faded and talkies took their place, Hayakawa turned for a time to theater. He toured the United States in several popular plays.

By the late 1930s the Hayakawas were living in Paris, France. He had made a few European films and was earning a living painting on silk. He and his wife were living modestly in the city, without a hint of the old Hollywood extravagance.

In 1940 the German army occupied Paris. Although Japan was an ally of Germany, he remained on the side of the European countries and their allies. Because of his wartime stance, the Hayakawas did not return to Japan until long after the war's end. In 1949 they went back to the United States where Hayakawa starred (with Humphrey Bogart) in a major Hollywood film called *Tokyo Joe*. A year later, he and his wife returned to Japan where he devoted himself to the study of Zen Buddhism, a religion that stresses meditation as a means of becoming enlightened. Eventually, he was chosen as a candidate for the priesthood and was ordained in a traditional Zen Buddhist ceremony.

Hayakawa's life of peaceful reflection was interrupted in 1956 when he briefly returned to acting. After much soul-searching concerning his religious beliefs about war and peace, he accepted a Hollywood movie contract to play the role of the Japanese colonel in the movie *The Bridge on the River Kwai* (1957). The role eventually won him an acclaimed Oscar nomination for best supporting actor.

Hayakawa made several more films before he returned to Japan in 1961 after the death of his wife. Once again he immersed himself in Zen Buddhism, living the remainder of his life in a modest home in suburban Tokyo, near his three grown children.

Sessue Hayakawa's life, which was an expression of his spirituality and wide range of artistic talents, enriched others. Some critics question his portrayal of the Asian American male as a stern, rigid disciplinarian. Others agree, however, that the ultimate test of a movie role is not exclusively the image that is created on screen.

Pablo Manlapit

Filipino Labor Leader
1891–1969

Filipino American workers of the early twentieth century differed from their Chinese and Japanese counterparts in one important way. When the United States took possession of the Philippine Islands after the Spanish-American War in 1898, the American government granted all Filipinos the status of American nationals. This meant that they would have most of the rights of U.S. citizens, except the rights to vote and to legally become citizens.

Because the Philippines was a U.S. protectorate, the U.S. government funded the education of Filipino children. They studied English and American history and culture. Later, when Filipino workers came to America seeking opportunity, they considered themselves like other Americans coming to the mainland. Unfortunately, as soon as they arrived, Filipinos met with prejudice and discrimination. Feeling betrayed, many were outraged by their treatment. A few men, like Pablo Manlapit, expressed their anger openly and began to organize workers to gain their rights.

Pablo Manlapit was born in 1891 in Lipa, Batangas, in the Philippines. After completing a few years of high school, he headed for Hawaii in 1910. In Hawaii, Manlapit went to work for the Hawaiian Sugar Planters' Association. His energy and hard work gained him quick promotions until his boss discovered that he was involved in a labor dispute. Then he was fired immediately.

Manlapit then left the plantation and moved to Hilo, where he started two newspapers and opened a pool hall. Later, while working as a janitor in a law office, he decided to study law. In 1919 he became the first Filipino in Hawaii to pass the bar examination. Manlapit used his skills as a lawyer to become a formidable foe of the plantation owners. In August 1919 he established the Filipino Federation of Labor and the following year organized the Filipino Higher Wage movement to improve living conditions among Filipino plantation workers. He worked tirelessly to increase workers' wages from 72¢ to $1.25 for an eight-hour day; to require overtime pay for work on Sundays and holidays; and to gain eight weeks of maternity leave with pay for women laborers. When the planters' association flatly rejected these demands, Manlapit called for a strike. On January 19, 1920, more than 3,000 Filipino and Japanese workers went on strike.

Sugar plantation owners fought hard to squelch the strike and eventually evicted 12,000 workers from plantation houses. The Hawaiian Sugar Planters' Association then called in strikebreakers and tried to prevent the workers' children from attending the local school. The pressure placed on the strikers was so great that, by the summer of 1920, all but 500 workers had returned to work. Altogether the strike lasted 165 days.

Between 1920 and 1924 Manlapit continued to organize workers. In April 1924 another strike took place on Oahu. This became the bloodiest day of labor unrest in Hawaii's history. Sixteen strikers and four policemen were killed in a skirmish that was called the Hanapepe Massacre.

Pablo Manlapit received a stiff prison sentence for his involvement in the incident but fled into exile rather than serve time. He resurfaced in Hawaii in 1932 and formed the Filipino Labor Union. By 1935, however, he was again on the run. This time he left Hawaii for good and lived out his life in the Philippines.

James Wong Howe

Cinematographer
1899–1976

"Good with his fists" is the way schoolmates described Jimmie Wong. So good, in fact, that when, after a few too many fights, he was asked to leave school, he became a boxer. By the time Wong was seventeen, however, he had left the ring and begun looking for work as a Hollywood cameraman. Many years later, when James Wong Howe was asked about his love for both boxing and filming movies, he said they are really quite similar: "You've got to duck. You've got to move fast. You've got to use your noodle."[10]

Born in Guangzhou, China, in 1899, Jimmie Wong moved with his family to Pasco, Washington, when he was just five. While his father worked hard to become a successful businessman—at one time he owned two restaurants, four hog ranches, a grocery store, a hardware store, and a great deal of real estate—Jimmie struggled as the only Chinese at an American school. As he remembered it, he did not like his classmates any better than they liked him.

After leaving school, he gained attention as the only Chinese boxer in the United States at the time. He traveled throughout the Northwest and down the Pacific Coast to California. One day, in Los Angeles, he came upon the filming of a Mack Sennett comedy in a city park. He was fascinated and decided soon afterward to quit boxing and get into the very young motion-picture industry.

A fellow boxer-turned-cameraman helped Jimmie Wong find a job as an errand boy with the Cecil B. DeMille studio. Wong soon realized that if he, too, wanted to film movies, he would need to first learn commercial photography. So he bought a camera and learned everything he could about both the technology and the art of photography. He asked every actress and actor he met if he could take their pictures. Within a few years he had truly become an expert with a camera.

James Wong Howe's career moved slowly at first, largely because of racial discrimination. (In fact, he used the last name Howe—his father's American first name—as a way of seeming less foreign.) As he recalled, "I was supposed to stick in the background and accept a certain number of insults." He had to make do with the worst equipment. Despite these conditions, Jimmie performed such wonders with a camera that he was finally given a studio contract. In 1923 he was director of photography on the silent film *The Trail of the Lonesome Pine.*

Once under contract, Jimmie Wong worked with great success on movie after movie and easily adjusted to the change from silent pictures to talkies. He worked with such major stars of early sound motion pictures as Marlene Dietrich, Gloria Swanson, and Joan Crawford. He was much favored by actresses because of his beautifully lit close-up shots, which always made them look extraordinarily beautiful on the big screen.

By the 1940s he was the best-paid cameraman in Hollywood and was considered one of the greatest cameramen in the world. Film offers came one after another and, eventually, Academy Award nominations, too. He was nominated sixteen times for an Oscar and won twice, once in 1955 for *The Rose Tattoo* and again in 1963 for *Hud,* starring Paul Newman. Other well-known films of Howe's include *The Charge of the Light Brigade* (1936), *Yankee Doodle Dandy* (1942), *Come Back, Little Sheba* (1952), and *The Old Man and the Sea* (1958). James Wong Howe died in Hollywood in 1976.

Dalip Singh Saund

Member, U.S. House of Representatives
1899–1973

Dalip S. Saund set his sights high and then reached even higher. As a graduate student in India, he rejected offers to join that country's tradition-bound civil service. He wished instead to follow the ideals of Abraham Lincoln and Woodrow Wilson, and so he moved to the United States. There his goal became nothing less than becoming "a living example of American democracy in practice."

Born to a wealthy landowner in northern India's Punjab Province, Saund was taught by his parents to respect learning. Because Saund's father saw the limitations placed on his own life by illiteracy, he felt strongly that his children should have the schooling they needed. Dalip Saund began school at an early age and then attended a local college before traveling to the University of the Punjab.

After rejecting offers for government work in India, Dalip Saund emigrated to the United States to continue his studies. In 1920 he enrolled in the graduate program in mathematics at the University of California, Berkeley. Two years later he received his M.A. degree, followed by a Ph.D. in 1924. While a student at Berkeley, he attended religious services at a Sikh temple in Stockton, California, where he met many fellow Hindus who farmed in the San Joaquin. After graduating he decided to farm with them, devoting his considerable intelligence and energy to his new vocation.

Within a short time, Saund became interested in politics. Unfortunately, according to U.S. immigration laws at the time, Asian Indians could not become American citizens. Without citizenship, Dalip Saund could not run for elected office. Instead he helped organize the India Association of America, which sent him to Washington, D.C., to urge an amendment to the anti-Asian immigration laws.

Dalip Singh Saund had always wanted to become an American citizen. He was, after all, married to an American and the father of three American children. It was only natural, he believed, that he should resent not being able to become a citizen of the United States.

When Congress passed the amendment to the immigration law in 1946, Saund immediately applied for citizenship. After his first full year as a citizen, he became a candidate for a judgeship in Westmoreland, California. To his great frustration, he was again declared ineligible, this time for not having been a citizen long enough!

Finally, in 1955, Saund made his first run for a seat in the U.S. House of Representatives, hoping to represent the huge 29th Congressional District, which extends from the Los Angeles suburbs to the Mexican border. He set the stakes high, stating that a vote for him would show there was no true prejudice in the United States. He defeated a popular Republican candidate by a few thousand votes.

When he was sworn in, he became the first Asian American elected to Congress. He was appointed to the influential House Foreign Affairs Committee, where he continued to concern himself with Asian, particularly Indian, matters. He made a well-publicized tour of India and addressed a joint session of India's House of Parliament. He forcefully advocated increasing cultural and educational exchanges between the two countries.

Congressman Saund was reelected twice. In the midst of his third campaign, in 1962, he was crippled by a massive stroke. Although he continued to campaign from his hospital bed, he lost this last bid for reelection. He never fully recovered from his debilitating stroke and died at his home in Hollywood in 1973.

Isamu Noguchi

Sculptor
1904–1988

The great artist and sculptor Isamu Noguchi resisted artistic boundaries and their limitations and experimented freely with stone, metal, wood, paper, and clay.

Isamu Noguchi was born in Los Angeles, California, in 1904. His Japanese father, Yone Noguchi, was a poet and art critic. His mother, Leonie Gilmour, was an American writer. At the time of Noguchi's birth, his father had already abandoned his mother and returned to Japan. Two years later, Noguchi and his mother left America and also moved to Japan to join him.

When Isamu Noguchi was seven, he and his mother moved to the seaside village of Chigasaki. In 1913, however, his father settled into a traditional marriage with a Japanese woman. In 1918 Noguchi's mother decided her son should go to America to continue his education. She enrolled him at Interlaken, an experimental school in northern Indiana. At thirteen, Noguchi made the trip to the States alone and arrived in the town of Rolling Prairie, only to find that the school had been closed and its property taken over by the U.S. Army as a training camp. Within the year, World War I ended and the camp was closed. Noguchi, having nowhere to go, joined two caretakers who were camping out in one of the deserted buildings.

Eventually Isamu Noguchi started attending a nearby public school. A year later Dr. Edward A. Rumely, founder of Interlaken, learned of Noguchi's dilemma and found a family that would take him in.

After high school graduation, the young artist apprenticed for a short time with Gutzon Borglum, an American sculptor best known for creating the Mount Rushmore National Memorial in South Dakota. The relationship between Borglum and Noguchi began to fail, however, shortly after Borglum told Noguchi that he would never become a true sculptor.

Disappointed by the rejection, Noguchi enrolled at New York's Columbia University in 1923, where he began studying medicine. In 1926, however, after seeing an exhibition of a Romanian sculptor, Constantin Brancusi, Noguchi decided to devote himself to art and discontinued his medical studies. A year later, in 1927, he received a Guggenheim Fellowship, which would allow him to study in Paris, France.

In Paris, Noguchi met Brancusi who, after a little persuasion, agreed to let him be his stonecutter. With Brancusi as his tutor, Noguchi learned to respect the materials and tools of the sculptor. In 1929 he left Paris and traveled throughout Asia. He spent time in Beijing, China, where he learned brush drawing. Later, he studied ceramics in Japan. By the time he returned to New York in the mid-1930s, his reputation as a sculptor was widely known.

Noguchi's fame spread nationally in 1938 when his design of a plaque was chosen for the new headquarters of the Associated Press at New York

City's Rockefeller Center. The plaque, which he had convinced sponsors to let him make in stainless steel, was unveiled in 1940 with great ceremony. The year before, Noguchi had thrilled New Yorkers with his "strikingly modern" fountain, which he had designed for the Ford Motor Company building at the New York World's Fair.

It appeared that Noguchi was well on his way in the art world. However, tragic world events in 1941 would reshape his life and force him to deal with the realities of his Japanese American citizenship.

On December 7, 1941, Japanese forces bombed Pearl Harbor in Hawaii. President Franklin Roosevelt immediately ordered the internment of Japanese Americans living on the West Coast. Although Isamu Noguchi lived in New York and was considered a "safe Japanese," he voluntarily went with other Japanese Americans to an internment camp in Poston, Arizona. His intention was to lend his skills in building playgrounds and parks for the inmates of the camp. Noguchi's intentions, however, were not welcomed by the War Relocation Authority. When Noguchi realized that his presence was not wanted, he applied for release from the camp.

Following his release from Poston seven months later, Noguchi began producing his most serious work to date. In 1952 he moved to Japan, where he married Yoshiko (Shirley) Yamaguchi. From their home in Japan and from a studio that he maintained in New York, Noguchi produced a marvelous array of stone, metal, wood, and paper sculptures, many of which were installed in public places around the world. He also began designing the sculpture gardens that are now prominent in such cities as New York, Houston, Los Angeles, and Jerusalem, and children's playgrounds in New York and Tokyo. These peaceful gardens and playgrounds, dotted with Noguchi's work, have helped bring—in the words of one art critic—"20th century sculpture into the realm of everyday life."

In 1985, just three years before his death, Isamu Noguchi opened the

Isamu Noguchi Garden Museum in a former factory in Long Island City, New York. Today, this unusual museum houses 200 examples of Noguchi's work, representing all the important influences on his art. Many of the pieces are carved from the stone of Japan's Shikoku Island, where Noguchi spent part of each year. Others are made from clay, wood, or other stone, which Isamu Noguchi believed contained all the energies of nature.

On Isamu Noguchi's application for the Guggenheim Fellowship in 1926, he wrote: "It is my desire to view nature through nature's eyes, and to ignore man as an object for special veneration. There must be unthought-of heights of beauty to which sculpture may be raised by his reversal of attitude."[11] Without a doubt, Isamu Noguchi has raised sculpture to unthought-of heights of beauty. Now others can think these thoughts and go beyond.

Philip Vera Cruz

Labor Leader
1904–1994

Philip Vera Cruz was born on Christmas Day 1904 in a small barrio called Saoang, in the province of Ilocos Sur, which is on the island of Luzon in the Philippines. Twenty-two years later, in 1926, he arrived in Seattle, Washington, in search of a better life.

He came for the same reasons other young Filipino men had come—to work, save money, and support their families. Soon after arriving in America, however, they learned just how difficult it would be to achieve their goals. As Philip Cruz remembered, "All the stories we heard were only success stories. So my plan was to finish college in America, get a good job over there, save my money, and then return home and support my family. It was only after I finally got to America that I understood how different reality was for us Filipinos."

Filipino men learned that reality meant low-paying jobs and racial discrimination. Conditions such as these led Filipino Americans who were working in the fields and canneries in Hawaii and on the West Coast of the United States to organize into unions to protect their rights and get better wages. Throughout the 1920s labor organizers such as Pablo Manlapit struggled to acquire better working conditions on the Hawaiian Islands. Others, such as Chris Mensalvas, Ernesto Mangaoang, and Larry Itliong, worked on the mainland from the 1930s to the 1960s to improve the quality of life for Filipino workers.

It was during the Filipino American farm laborers' strike in the asparagus fields of Stockton, California, that Philip Cruz first met Chris Mensalvas. And it was there that Philip Cruz first dedicated himself to the cause of Filipino labor rights. Although Cruz would like to have stayed on to help the union, he was financially desperate. Feeling obligated to help support his family, especially his younger brother who was in law school in Manila, Philip Cruz went on to Alaska to work in a salmon cannery.

In Alaska workers were protected by a strong union. Conditions and pay were better than California standards. But work lasted only for two summer months. So it was back to California—to Delano where grapes needed to be picked. By that time the Stockton strike was over. Although the strike had brought Filipino American workers together, it would take another twenty years before they would unite again in such numbers for a common cause. This time it would be in the grape fields south of Stockton—back in Delano.

For the next twenty years Philip Vera Cruz continued traveling with migrant groups, working at seasonal jobs in fields and canneries throughout the western United States. On September 8, 1965, in Delano, he joined others in a grape strike that sparked the great farm workers movement of the 1960s and led to the historic formation of the United Farm Workers (UFW) under the charismatic leadership of Cesar Chavez.

During this strike Philip Cruz became an officer of the UFW. In 1971 he became its vice president, a position he held until his resignation in 1977. In 1987 he was awarded the first Ninoy M. Aquino Award for lifelong service to the Filipino community in America. The award included a trip back to the Philippines, the first he had made since leaving there sixty years before. There he was reunited with the family he had worked so hard to support over the years. As he later recalled, "My brother and sister got good educations and they succeeded in providing their children with a good education. That's important to me because I made it possible for them."

Philip Vera Cruz came to the United States to work, save money, and support his family. He achieved this goal and more. His efforts helped change history and improve the lives of thousands in the process. "If I could inspire one or two young people to be successful by hearing my story," he once said, ". . . if more young people could just get involved in the important issues of social justice, they would form a golden foundation for the struggle of all people to improve their lives."[12]

Anna May Wong

Actress
1905–1961

Mr. Wong always told Anna May Wong that becoming an actress was not a suitable profession for a proper Chinese daughter, but the headstrong teenager ignored her father. She snuck out of her family's home to visit casting agents in nearby Hollywood. Her father, who worked as a laundryman in Los Angeles and could barely support his large family, was outraged at her gumption. Despite the family's money woes, he would never agree to Anna's working in such a profession.

Anna May Wong appeared in a silent film called *The Red Lantern* when she was just fourteen. This role was followed by many other small parts, but the characters she was asked to play were always the same: sinister Oriental women with mysterious power over white men. These so-called dragon ladies are then rejected once the men find suitable white women. This theme, with its racist overtones, followed Anna May Wong from film to film. Her struggle to find good, respectable roles lasted her entire lifetime.

Some of the parts Wong played should have brought her recognition as a serious actress. In 1924 she starred in *The Thief of Baghdad* opposite the matinee idol Douglas Fairbanks. Once again she played an Oriental slave, but this time her beauty and talent caught the attention of movie audiences. Even so, although her fine features were breathtaking on camera and audiences loved her, Anna May Wong could not break the Hollywood screen image of the Chinese as evil and untrustworthy. She begged for better roles so, when none were offered to her, she left the United States.

In Europe, Anna May Wong was treated as a serious actress. She made several films in Germany during the late 1920s and 1930s and became a popular star. When talking pictures replaced silent ones, she studied German and French and was able to speak fluently in her films. In an effort to mold herself into an all-around talent, she began singing and dancing. In 1929 Anna May Wong acted opposite the great English actor Sir Lawrence Olivier in a play called *The Circle of Chalk*.

When Anna May Wong returned to the United States in 1930, however, Fu Manchu movies were the rage. The movie character Dr. Fu Manchu, based on the character created by novelist Saxe Rohmer, was an evil Chinese doctor who plotted to take over Europe and America. The Fu Manchu novels called this notion "the yellow menace," and it helped feed the prejudices of many Americans. Anna May Wong was not proud when she accepted parts in such films as *Daughter of the Dragon* (1931) and *Daughter of Shanghai* (1937), but she had no choice if she wanted to work in Hollywood.

In 1936, when Wong visited China for the first time, she was publicly criticized for taking such roles. She tried to explain that in Hollywood "good" Chinese parts are played by whites and the evil ones by Asians. The casting of the 1937 film *The Good Earth,* based on the best-selling novel by Pearl S. Buck, was just one example of this discriminatory practice. Anna May Wong fought hard for the lead role in that film and was bitterly disappointed when it was given to a white actress.

Hollywood did begin to change but only slowly. After the Japanese invaded China in 1937, American moviemakers saw the value of portraying the Chinese in a more generous way. Anna May Wong was finally offered better movie roles. She also worked hard for various Chinese relief organizations and funds and entertained U.S. troops overseas during World War II.

After the war, however, Anna May Wong was largely forgotten by Hollywood producers. Her lifelong struggle to become a respected film actress failed simply for lack of opportunity. Despite her pioneering efforts to create better roles for Asians, when she died in 1961, she was remembered by *Time* magazine as a "foremost Hollywood villainess."

S. I. Hayakawa

U.S. Senator, Scholar, College President
1906–1992

Controversy surrounded Samuel Ichiye Hayakawa wherever he went. He seemed to thrive on it. From 1941, when as a young linguistics professor he published his landmark book *Language in Action,* through his days as president of San Francisco State University, to his one term in the U.S. Senate, he never worried about what others thought of him.

S.I. Hayakawa was born in Vancouver, British Columbia, Canada, in 1906, where his father ran an import-export business. In 1930, after his family had returned to Japan, Hayakawa headed for Madison, Wisconsin, to pursue a doctoral degree in language arts at the University of Wisconsin. After graduating in 1935, he accepted a position as professor of semantics (the study of word meaning and usage) and taught courses first at the

University of Wisconsin in Madison and then at the Illinois Institute of Technology in Chicago.

Hayakawa learned to balance his time between teaching and writing. In 1941 he published his first book, called *Language in Action*. It was the first book to be written about language for a wide audience and soon became a national best-seller. It offered an explanation as to why and how people react to words and language and was based in part on studies of how Nazi leaders used language to manipulate people and gain political control of Germany in the 1930s.

By the time Hayakawa left Chicago in 1955 for a professorship in language arts at San Francisco State College, his reputation as a linguistics scholar was already well established. For more than ten years he lectured at San Francisco State while finding time to write three more books and to lecture widely.

In 1968, during a critical time at San Francisco State, Hayakawa was named its president. Student demonstrators, upset over the firing of an African American instructor, were in the midst of striking to shut down the school. Hayakawa acted quickly to oppose the strike and had more than 400 protesters arrested. Newspapers carried photographs of him nationwide, wearing his trademark hat (a woolen cap of Scottish origin called a tam o'shanter) and tearing out wires of the sound system that students were using to express their views.

For some students Hayakawa symbolized parental authority gone mad. Many Asian Americans opposed his tactics and were embarrassed by him. For others he symbolized what a courageous, no-nonsense leader should be. It was upon these people that he would rely for support in his bid for a seat in the U.S. Senate eight years later.

In 1976 Hayakawa turned his attention to politics as the Republican candidate for the U.S. Senate. He ran against the incumbent, John Tunney, and won in a close race. In the Senate, Hayakawa became one of the most conservative members, opposing affirmative action and busing to achieve racial integration. He favored a constitutional amendment making English the official language of the United States.

After three years the Californians who had supported Hayakawa and sent him to the Senate were tired of his laid-back style of leadership. They would not tolerate his falling asleep during Senate proceedings and his characterization as "Sleepin' Sam" by the press. When it came time for him to run for a second term in 1982, many of his conservative supporters abandoned him. As a result, he quickly dropped out of the race.

Returning to his home in Mill Valley, California, Hayakawa continued to campaign against bilingualism (the use of two languages) in his home state. Believing that "the most rapid way to get out of a ghetto is to speak good English," he formed the California English Campaign, which in 1986 succeeded in making English the state's official language.

Samuel Ichiye Hayakawa, scholar, college president, and U.S. Senator, died on February 27, 1992. He will best be remembered for his pioneering work in the field of semantics.

Hiram Leong Fong

U.S. Senator
1906–

At age seven, Hiram Fong was already earning a living by selling newspapers, catching fish and crabs, and picking mesquite beans. As one of eleven children of Chinese-born workers on a Hawaiian sugar plantation, Hiram could scarcely hope for more than a life of fieldwork himself. But brains and ambition helped this boy get out of the slums of Kalihi, Hawaii, and into the halls of the U.S. Capitol in Washington, D.C.

Lum Fong and his wife, Chai Ha Lum, had been in Hawaii nearly thirty years before their son Hiram was born in 1906. They had both come from China's Kwangtung Province as indentured servants. By the time Hiram was born, Lum Fong was earning $12 a month. His wife, who worked alongside him in the fields, earned nothing. Their children quickly learned that they, too, had to work to help put food on the family's table.

Hiram Fong attended public school near the sugar plantation. He did very well and went on to be accepted at the University of Hawaii. Lack of money, however, forced him to delay going to college. He worked for three years as a clerk at the Pearl Harbor Naval Shipyard until he had saved enough money for tuition. Once he was finally enrolled at the university, he completed four years of classwork in three, graduating with highest honors. But there was time also for more than academics. Fong was an active member of the volleyball, debate, and rifle teams and served as editor of the student newspaper. He also held a part-time job to earn money for law school and in 1932 entered Harvard University.

In 1935 Hiram returned home to Honolulu from Cambridge, Massachusetts, with a Harvard law degree and ten cents in his pocket. He began practicing law, eventually founding Honolulu's first multiracial law firm of Fong, Miho, Choy & Robinson (with Chinese, Japanese, Korean, and white American partners). Hiram Fong's law practice prospered and his own financial investments became so lucrative that within a few years he became a millionaire.

Financial security freed Fong to follow his political interests. He was first elected to the legislature of the territory of Hawaii in 1938 and served for fourteen years. In 1942 he became vice speaker of the House of Representatives and later Speaker of the House. In 1950 he became vice president of the Territorial Constitutional Convention and in that position helped bring statehood to Hawaii in 1959.

When Hawaiians voted on June 27, 1959, to bring statehood to the islands, they also voted in a primary election for seats in the U.S. Congress. Hiram Fong ran unopposed as a Republican candidate for the U.S. Senate.

During the elections for state representatives at the end of July, four men were chosen to go to Washington. By winning a coin toss, Hiram Fong became the new state's senior U.S. Senator.

Considered by many to be one of Hawaii's most popular elected officials, Hiram Fong was overwhelmingly reelected to the Senate in 1964. He retired from the Senate in 1977 and has since lived in Honolulu with his wife of more than sixty years. Now in his nineties, he spends part of each day weeding and trimming at Senator Fong's Plantation and Gardens. This 725-acre (293 hectare) nature park on the island of Oahu is open to the public and welcomes thousands of visitors each year. The gardens are Hiram Fong's last gift to his beloved Hawaii.

Toshio Mori

Writer
1910–1980

Even though Toshio Mori played baseball well enough to try out with the Chicago Cubs, there was never any doubt that his dream of becoming a writer took first place in his life. Born in California to Japanese parents, Mori became Americanized at an early age. Although he had only a high school education, he continued learning on his own. Frequenting libraries and bookstores, he saturated his mind with literature and ideas whenever he could. Although he worked twelve hours a day in the family-owned plant nursery and flower shop in rural San Leandro, California, Toshio disciplined himself to write for four hours each night, because he wanted to become a writer. For twenty years he worked so hard he thought his weariness would one day cause him to "fall by the wayside." But his determination paid off.

In 1938, six years after starting full-time work at the nursery, Mori's first fictional story, about Japanese America, was published. By 1941 his stories were being printed in six national literary journals and had caught the attention of the well-known writer William Saroyan, who considered Mori "a natural born writer" and "the first real Japanese-American writer."

At the close of 1941, a collection of his short stories was scheduled to go to press. The Japanese attack of the American naval base in Hawaii on December 7, however, halted the printing of the book, and it was not published until eight years later, under the title *Yokohama, California*. The stories, which depict the lives of Japanese Americans in California, are written from the heart.

After the bombing of Pearl Harbor, Toshio Mori and his family were among 120,000 other Japanese Americans to be removed from their homes and sent to live in concentration camps for the remainder of World War II. Hopeful that his writing career would become successful one day, Mori kept writing during his internment at the Topaz internment camp in Utah.

When the war ended and he returned to his family's home in San Leandro, he intended to recover more than two hundred of the stories he had hurriedly stored in a barn when the government imprisoned his family several years before. But the stories had been destroyed by bookworms. Mori's career never quite recovered from this setback, and for the next thirty years his work remained unrecognized.

In the late 1970s, a new generation of Japanese Americans briefly discovered the value of Toshio Mori's stories, and new attention was given to his work. They considered his fiction a humorous, yet respectful, look at the lives of the Issei (first-generation Japanese immigrants) of the early twentieth century. For his contribution to the Japanese American community, Mori was honored at Asian American Writers' conferences in Oakland, Seattle, and Honolulu. In 1979 the UCLA Asian American Studies Center published an anthology of his work called *The Chauvinist and Other Stories*.

During his long career, Mori wrote hundreds of short stories and six novels, the vast majority of which have yet to be published. It is unfortunate that, because of discrimination, his writing was not taken seriously by the literary community. According to Saroyan in 1949, Toshio Mori was probably "one of the most important new writers in the country at the moment."

Bienvenido N. Santos

Writer
1911–1996

"Each time I left the United States for the Philippines, I thought I was going for good," wrote Ben Santos in the preface to his collection of short stories, *Scent of Apples*. Instead, he kept returning and eventually became a U.S. citizen. Over the years Santos's life took on the shape of the Filipino American experience he depicted so well in his stories. In fact, he once said, "Sometimes I cannot distinguish between these characters and the real persons I have known in America. The years have a way of distorting memories. Now, too, our coming and going appear to have taken the shape of my characters' predicaments. Like those who carry memories as a burden, I find it more and more impossible to travel light."

Bienvenido Nuqui Santos was born in the Philippine capital of Manila in 1911 and grew up in the Tondo, an infamous slum district. At the time, the Philippine Islands were a protectorate of the United States, and Filipino citizens were given the status of United States nationals. That meant that although they had most of the rights and privileges of U.S. citizens, they could not vote in American elections or become citizens.

As a boy growing up in the Philippines, Santos was educated in schools that used American textbooks and followed American customs. He learned "The Star-Spangled Banner" and was taught by American or American-trained teachers.

In 1941 he graduated from the University of the Philippines. Then as a *pensionado,* a scholarship student chosen by the commonwealth government to study abroad in return for a commitment to public service upon his return, Santos came to the U.S. mainland to study at the University of Illinois, where he eventually received his master's degree.

When Japanese armies occupied the Philippines soon after the United States entered World War II, Santos and many of his fellow countrymen were stranded in the States. They naturally gravitated toward the Commonwealth Government in Exile in Washington, D.C., for which some people, like Santos, acted as spokesmen for the cause of the Philippines throughout the United States. When Ben Santos returned to the Philippines after World War II, he was "full of stories about his lonely and lost fellow exiles in America." Later he wrote a collection of short stories called *You Lovely People,* which portrays the lives of these lonely, wandering men.

In 1972 Ferdinand Marcos, president of the Philippine Islands, imposed martial law in the Philippines and temporarily closed schools. Ben Santos, who was in the States at the time, could not return to teach. Instead he took a position at Wichita State University, where he taught English and became their Distinguished Writer in Residence.

Ben Santos's published books include *Brother My Brother* (1960), *Villa Magdalena* (1965), and *Scent of Apples* (1980). Throughout his life Santos had traveled extensively, balancing a heavy schedule of writing, teaching, and lecturing throughout the United States and the Philippines. He died at his home in Albay, in the Philippines, in 1996.

Carlos Bulosan

Writer
1911–1956

"We arrived in Seattle on a June day. My first sight of the approaching land was an exhilarating experience. Everything seemed native and promising to me. It was like coming home after a long voyage, although as yet I had no home in this city." So wrote Carlos Bulosan, remembering his first sight, in 1930, of the America that was to be his home for the rest of his short life.

The Philippine Islands, which Carlos Bulosan had just left, had been a colonial territory of the United States since 1898, when the islands were ceded to the United States at the end of the Spanish-American War. Bulosan, unlike Asians from elsewhere, came to America as a United States national. This meant that these Filipino workers, or *pinoys,* as they were often called, had most of the rights and privileges of U. S. citizens, although they could not vote in American elections or become citizens.

Carlos Bulosan was born in 1911 in the village of Binalonan in Pangasinan Province. His parents were not poor by local standards; they had managed to put two sons through high school. Although Bulosan did not graduate from high school before he left for the United States mainland, he did spend a year or two in school where he first demonstrated his writing talent in English in the school newspaper.

Prior to the Americans coming to the Philippines, the islands had been a colony of Spain, and Spanish was the language of education and the small educated class. By the time Carlos Bulosan attended school, however, English had become the language of education in the Philippines. His textbooks were filled with stories of American heroes such as Presidents Washington and Lincoln and of the ideals of American democracy. He pledged allegiance to the American flag each day and was taught that he was the equal of any American anywhere. Bulosan, like all Filipinos, could freely come and go to the United States mainland. They were not restricted by immigration laws like other Asians were.

Because the life of a Philippine farmer was hard, it is not surprising that in the 1920s and 1930s, thousands of young men left home looking for fortune in the United States. The idea that you could get rich quick in the United States was reinforced by the stories told by returning pinoys who wore fancy clothes and flashed extra cash. Letters from America were always optimistic, too.

Driven by the lure of America, Carlos Bulosan's parents sold a portion of their land to raise the seventy-five dollars for his passage as they had for his two brothers before him. At the age of nineteen he left his family and the familiar countryside to join the tens of thousands of his countrymen who had already sailed to America.

Although there had been no legal barriers to Bulosan's coming into the United States, once he arrived in Seattle, Washington, he came face to face with the ugly realities of American racism. It was hard to accept the fact that the equality and opportunity he had dreamed of in America, indeed had been taught existed there, were not available to pinoys. Although he had been taught to think of himself as American, he felt more like an exile or even a criminal.

California laws, as well as those of many other states, discriminated against pinoys. They were not allowed to marry white women; they were disqualified from many jobs; and they were allowed to live only in segregated parts of cities. Pinoys could be cannery workers, dishwashers, house servants, or farm laborers, but little else. As a pinoy, Bulosan drifted from one job to the next and from one unemployment line to another. He joined the body of homeless men who followed the harvest from southern California to Washington State to Alaska and back. As job conditions worsened, Filipino workers began to organize into labor unions to try and change things. Carlos Bulosan threw his whole support behind the labor movement and the "progressive forces," as he called them, that drove it.

Soon he began writing about it. In 1932 he published his first book of poems. From then on, writing was to be his major occupation.

Bulosan lived with his brother Aurelio in Los Angeles and spent much of his time in the public library where he read extensively. By 1934 his writing began to gain prominence. Then in 1936 his world fell apart. He was diagnosed with tuberculosis and spent the next two years in Los Angeles County Hospital recuperating. He continued to read and to write. From his hospital bed he followed reports of World War II erupting in Spain, Europe, and Northeast Asia.

When the United States entered the war in 1941 and the Japanese invaded the Philippines, the attitude toward those of Philippine ancestry seemed to change. Once scorned and ignored, they were suddenly welcomed as comrades in the fight against facism. This change, in part, led to a greater interest in the works of Carlos Bulosan. He published two books of poetry—*Letter from America* in 1942 and *Voice of Bataan* in 1943. The following year his best-known book, *Laughter of My Father,* was published.

The book Bulosan is best remembered for today, *America Is in the Heart,* was published in 1946. It is an autobiographical novel in which he tells the story of the Filipino in America. And while he describes all the heartbreaks and frustrations, all the racism that faced the pinoy, the book ends with praise for America. It is not the America of racist oppression that is the real America, he says. Rather, the real America is still the America of his Philippine dreams, the ideal America that is in the heart.

> I glanced out of the window again to look at the broad land I had dreamed so much about, only to discover with astonishment that the American earth was like a huge heart unfolding warmly to receive me. . . . It came to me that no man—no one at all—could destroy my faith in America again. It was something that had grown out of my defeats and successes, something shaped by my struggles for a place in this vast land. . . . It was something that grew out of the sacrifices and loneliness of my friends, of my brothers in America and my family in the Philippines—something that grew out of our desire to know America and to become a part of her great tradition, and to contribute something toward her final fulfillment. I knew that no man could destroy my faith in America that had sprung from all our hopes and aspiration, ever.[13]

Bulosan was thirty-five years old when *America Is in the Heart* was first published. Ten years later, he died in Seattle, the city that had welcomed him to America. He died a young man in a body old before its time. In his final years he had continued to fight for the ideal America, working closely with the Filipino labor union, ILWU Local 37, where, among other things, he edited the yearbook and wrote poetry. Some thirty years later a committee made up of Filipino community members, former friends, and University of Washington students erected a tombstone at Bulosan's grave. The epitaph comes from one of his unpublished poems:

> Here, here the tomb of Bulosan is:
> Here, here also are his words,
> dry as the grass is.

Ahn Chang-Ho

Social Activist
1878–1938

Philip Ahn

Film and Television Actor
1905–1978

Ahn Chang-Ho

Through the efforts of Ahn Chang-Ho, Korean Americans were able to study wherever they wanted and reach for the highest career goals. It may have been something of a disappointment to him, therefore, when his own son, Philip, after graduating from the University of Southern California, decided to become a movie actor—a career not considered a proper choice for educated Koreans.

Philip Ahn in the movie Chinese Sky, *1945*

Ahn Chang-Ho was born in Kangso City, Korea, in 1878. There were few opportunities for bright young Koreans at the time, so, encouraged by American missionaries, Ahn came to study in California in 1903. He decided to postpone his graduate studies, however, after seeing firsthand the effects of racial discrimination on the Koreans living in the San Francisco Bay area. Thereafter, the sensitive young man devoted himself to improving the lives of his fellow countrymen, many of whom longed to return to a freer, more prosperous Korea.

Ahn joined a select group of Korean activists in America—one of whom was Syngman Rhee, who became president of the Republic of Korea in 1948. Ahn organized the first Korean community organization, called the

Friendship Society, and the first Korean political organization, the Mutual Assistance Society. The latter merged in 1909 with other groups to become the Korean National Association.

When Japan annexed Korea in 1910, factions within the Korean American community could not agree on the best way to achieve Korea's independence. Ahn believed that Korea must first achieve spiritual rebirth. To this end, he made the heart-wrenching decision in the 1930s to leave his wife and children in California and return to Korea. He was later captured by the Japanese and sent to prison, where, after being tortured, he died on March 10, 1938.

Philip Ahn, born in Highland Park, California, in 1905, never knew his father well. To the young boy, his father was a stern but loving man whose lofty reputation cast a shadow on the rest of the family. When Ahn disapproved of Philip's dream to become an actor, Philip replied that he could never be expected to match his great father's expectations.

With Ahn gone for much of Philip's childhood, the presence of Hollywood's growing film industry influenced him more than his father's political work. Philip finished college, as his father had wished, but began his film career as soon as classes were over.

In his lifetime Philip Ahn appeared in more than 300 films, playing a range of Asian characters. His thirty-year career included roles in some of Hollywood's best-known pictures. From *The General Died at Dawn* (1936) to *The Good Earth*, and *Love Is a Many-Splendored Thing*, the versatile actor made his mark on American movies.

In many ways Philip Ahn's Hollywood career mirrored that of other Asian American actors. He, like Anna May Wong, was often criticized for accepting roles that showed Asians in a negative light. Philip Ahn portrayed Japanese and Chinese villains in many war pictures from the 1940s and 1950s. He appeared opposite the all-American hero John Wayne in *Halls of*

Montezuma, Battle Zone, and *Battle Hymn.* His response to criticism about these roles was the same as Ms. Wong's. "There is no choice," he would say. "I either take these parts or stop acting altogether."

The Hollywood Chamber of Commerce recognized Philip Ahn's contributions to moviemaking by inscribing his name in their well-known "Walk of Fame." He thus became the first Asian actor so honored. He also became well known for his starring role as Master Kan in the television series *Kung Fu,* in which he portrayed a teacher in a Chinese monastery preparing young students to master the wisdom and movements of kung fu.

As Philip Ahn grew older, however, he thought more and more about his father's legacy. He read and studied all he could about the days before Korea's independence in 1945. At the time of his death in 1978, he was preparing to travel to Seoul, South Korea, to honor the memory of his father, Ahn Chang-Ho, the spiritual and intellectual leader of the early Korean American community.

Chien-Shiung Wu

Nuclear Physicist
1912–1997

When Chien-Shiung Wu first decided to come to the United States to attend graduate school to study physics, she planned to enroll at the University of Michigan. But when she found out that 500 other students from China were enrolled there, she chose another school, the University of California at Berkeley, where the Chinese students were American-born. Surrounded by fellow countrymen, she worried that she might become lazy and not learn as much as she could about America and its way of life at Michigan.

Madame Wu, the eminent physicist, as called by her students and colleagues, was born in Liu Ho, China. Her father was a school principal, and he encouraged his three children to read widely and explore the world around them. Chien-Shiung Wu especially loved solving puzzles, and when she entered the National Central University in Shanghai, she expected to become a mathematician. But work on X rays for a senior thesis convinced her that the study of matter and energy and the interactions between them—physics—would become her life's work.

In the late 1930s and early 1940s, the science of physics was advancing at a dizzying speed. One Berkeley professor, Ernest Lawrence, had just invented a new machine called the cyclotron, which could smash atoms. Two German scientists had recently discovered that an atom of uranium split in half released huge amounts of energy. Uranium fission, as this was called, greatly interested Madame Wu, who undertook experiments to discover its possibilities.

At Berkeley in 1939, the physicist Robert Oppenheimer asked Madame Wu to give a seminar on the subject of fission. During her talk to colleagues she discussed the possibility of a chain reaction—atoms splitting one after the other, creating a huge explosion. It would clearly be a catastrophe, she said. A few years later she worked on the famous Manhattan Project, which led to the invention and development of the atomic bomb.

In 1942 Dr. Wu married another physicist, Luke Yuan, and the couple began a commuting relationship between her teaching and research at Columbia University and Dr. Yuan's work in Princeton, New Jersey. A son, Vincent, was born to the couple in 1947.

Madame Wu soon began experiments on a form of radioactivity called beta decay. She stunned her colleagues by obtaining precise measurements of subatomic particles. In fact, her measurements were so exact that she soon gained a reputation for never making a mistake.

In the 1950s two fellow Chinese physicists, Tsung Dao Lee of Columbia University and Chen Ning Yang of Princeton, challenged one of the basic laws of physics, the law of conservation of parity. (Their story is given later in this book.) This law states that if you perform an experiment and then repeat it, doing everything the same way but reversing left and right, you will obtain the same results. Physicists believed so deeply in the idea that nature does not know her left hand from her right that no one had ever considered challenging it.

Drs. Lee and Yang, however, wrote that under some circumstances this law does not hold up. Using the experiments of Madame Wu, the two were able to announce to the world, in 1957, that their results rejected what was considered an established fact of nature. That year, Drs. Lee and Yang were rewarded for their boldness with the Nobel Prize in Physics. Madame Wu was honored by the National Academy of Sciences and many other inter-national science organizations.

In later years Dr. Wu researched so-called exotic atoms, using nuclear physics to find the cause of such diseases as sickle-cell anemia. In studies of radioactive substances at very low temperatures and at great depths in the earth, Madame Wu and several colleagues spent long periods at the bottom of a 2,000-foot (609 m) salt mine near Cleveland, Ohio. One colleague recalled the sight of Madame Wu emerging from the mine, looking lovely in her traditional silk Chinese dress, smiling broadly at the sight of the bright sun.

Madame Wu retired from teaching at Columbia in 1982 and often spoke and wrote about the place of women in the sciences and in physics in particular. She also traveled the world, collecting awards and honorary doctoral degrees. In 1990 the Chinese Academy of Science named a star for Chien-Shiung Wu, the first time they had so honored a living person. She died in 1997.

Minoru Yamasaki

Architect
1912–1986

When twenty-two-year-old Minoru Yamasaki arrived in New York from his hometown of Seattle, Washington, he had forty dollars to his name and a few bleak prospects for work. The bustling city seemed at first no place for this shy, second-generation Japanese American. Yamasaki, however, would eventually leave his mark on this dynamic city. In 1973 he would design the twin towers of the World Trade Center, which architecturally dominated the skyline of Lower Manhattan for the next twenty-eight years.

When Minoru was a teenager, he decided to become an architect. He made his decision soon after seeing drawings of the U.S. embassy in Tokyo, which his uncle, architect Koken Ito, had designed. Minoru enrolled at the University of Washington in Seattle, where he earned a bachelor's degree in architecture in 1934. Thinking there would be less discrimination and racism against Asian Americans on the East Coast and more opportunities for him to advance his career, Minoru left his hometown and headed to New York City.

Yamasaki's first professional architecture assignment was with the New York firm of Githens and Keally. While working for the firm, Yamasaki began studying for a graduate degree in art and architecture at New York University. Eventually he became a part-time instructor at Columbia University in New York.

In 1949 he accepted a position with a large Detroit architecture firm and moved to Michigan, where he lived the rest of his life. Early in his career he specialized in large public projects, including the Urban Redevelopment Plan in St. Louis in 1952 and the St. Louis Airport Terminal Building in 1955. The latter design won him the American Institute of Architects' first honor award in 1956.

In time the pressure of undertaking such massive public projects nearly ruined Yamasaki's health. In the late 1950s he was hospitalized for ulcers and high blood pressure. "I realized there's a danger of an architect getting involved in too many things for the sake of society," he wrote, referring to his early years. "He's tempted to forget his real job is beauty."

Yamasaki's later designs reflected his desire to bring serenity, surprise, and grace to his work. "Delight," he told a group of architects in 1959, "must include the play of sun and shadow, a use of texture in materials to give pleasure, and the silhouetting of a building against the sky." His best-known designs are the Century Plaza Complex in Los Angeles; the U.S. Consulate in Kobe, Japan; Rainier Square in Seattle; and the World Trade Center Towers in New York, completed in 1973 but destroyed by terrorist attacks on September 11, 2001.

Spark Masayuki Matsunaga

U.S. Senator
1916–1990

Peace was Senator Spark Masayuki Matsunaga's main concern. As soon as he defeated Congresswoman Patsy Mink in 1976 for one of Hawaii's U.S. Senate seats, he became one of the strongest proponents of nuclear arms control in Washington, D.C. One of the bills he favored most would have created a National Academy of Peace.

Matsunaga was born in Kauai, Hawaii, in 1916. He excelled in school right from the start and, in 1941, graduated Phi Beta Kappa from the University of Hawaii. His goal had long been to attend law school, but after the Japanese bombing of Pearl Harbor, Hawaii, on December 7, 1941, his plans changed dramatically. Law school was postponed when he instead joined the army.

Matsunaga joined the 442nd Regimental Combat Team and, following very difficult training, was sent to Italy to fight against German and Italian forces—Japan's allies in the war. The regiment became one of the most celebrated of the war. For his bravery and for wounds in action as a member of the 442nd, Lieutenant Colonel Matsunaga received the Purple Heart.

After returning to the United States, Matsunaga won a scholarship to Harvard Law School, from which he graduated in 1951. He then moved back to Hawaii and served in the territorial legislature from 1952 to 1954. In 1959 he served in the new state's senate and established himself as one of Hawaii's most popular elected officials. He was elected to the U.S. Senate in 1976.

After arriving in Washington, D.C., in 1977, Senator Matsunaga became known for his support of legislation promoting peace and the environment. He also lobbied for an official apology by the U.S. government for the incarceration of Japanese Americans during World War II. He gave many impassioned speeches on the Senate floor, often invoking the memory of an elderly Issei who crossed an internment camp fence to retrieve a ball for a grandchild and was shot to death.

Senator Matsunaga's efforts to gain retribution for detention camp survivors were rewarded. In 1988 President Reagan officially apologized to Japanese Americans and issued payment of $20,000 to each of the survivors of the internment camps. Spark Matsunaga served in the U.S. Senate until his death from cancer in 1990.

I.M. Pei

Architect
1917–

A s a college student visiting the United States for the first time in the 1930s, I.M. Pei could not help but notice that America's urban landscape was pretty dull. Most new construction, whether for offices or museums or airport terminals, was practical and nondescript. Even then this young man, bursting with new ideas, was bold enough to believe that he might one day leave his own imprint on these sprawling modern cities.

Ieoh Ming Pei was born in Canton, China, the eldest son of a wealthy banker. At ten, Pei and his family moved to the bustling city of Shanghai, where his father managed the Bank of China's main office. A building boom in Shanghai at this time provided Pei the opportunity to see his first high-rise building.

Pei was interested in architecture at an early age. By the time he was seventeen, he spoke English well and decided to study architecture in the United States. He arrived in 1935, studied briefly at the University of Pennsylvania, and then transferred to the Massachusetts Institute of Technology. He received his master's degree in architecture from Harvard University in 1946. By this time, the political situation in post–World War II China made it impossible for him to return home, so he joined an architectural firm in New York. When the Communists gained control of China in 1949, his stay in the U.S. became permanent. Pei became an American citizen in 1954.

I.M Pei and Partners of New York was founded in 1955. The company took on several large urban projects—research centers, museums, and hospitals—in such cities as New York, Denver, Philadelphia, and Montreal. By the early 1960s, the world had begun to take notice of Pei's bold new approach to architecture.

One of Pei's first projects to gain wide public notice was a huge steel and glass terminal for TWA at New York's JFK International Airport. Other projects have included Denver's Mile High Center, the Syracuse University School of Journalism, and Boston's John Hancock Building. This last construction, in the heart of Boston, almost sank Pei's firm when the blue-green windows of the sixty-story structure began popping out onto the street below. Finally, when the cause of this disaster was discovered to be badly manufactured glass, the reputation of I.M. Pei and Partners was rescued.

In 1978 Pei's unusual addition to the National Gallery of Art in Washington, D.C., restored his standing completely. The next year the John F. Kennedy Library in Boston also opened to glowing reviews by both visitors and architectural critics. That same year, 1979, Pei received the Gold Medal of the American Institute of Architects, architecture's highest award.

Yet Pei's grandest and most controversial project was still to come. In 1985 he was chosen by France's president François Mitterand to undertake an extension of the country's greatest national treasure, the Louvre Museum in Paris. Pei's design of a glass pyramid at first seemed in conflict with the grand style of this sixteenth-century palace. When Pei's drawings became public, there was an uproar in France. Many believed this radical new structure would mar the beauty of the world's most famous museum: however, when the building was completed in 1989, the public welcomed it warmly. One *New York Times* critic pronounced it "an exquisite object."

Pei's career seemed to come full circle when, in late 1989, he finished a seventy-story office tower for the Bank of China in Hong Kong. His own father had founded the Hong Kong branch in 1919, and Pei tried bringing together the various influences on his own life—the traditional Chinese and the radically modern American. He was deeply saddened, though, when, in June 1989, the Chinese government's massacre of students at Beijing's Tiananmen Square showed that the new China was not as open and modern as his design might suggest.

In 1990 Pei retired from active involvement with his architectural firm. He has worked nonetheless on two important projects: the Rock and Roll Hall of Fame in Cleveland, Ohio (1995) and the Miho Museum in Kyoto, Japan (1998). When not causing a stir somewhere around the world, Pei lives in New York City with his wife of fifty years. To Pei's great happiness, two of his four children have joined his firm and work such as he did to change both the look and outlook of the entire world.

Joyce Chen

Chef, Restaurateur, Businesswoman
1918–1994

When Joyce Chen was a young girl in Beijing, China, she liked to spend hours watching her family's chef prepare classical Mandarin dishes. She stood beside the thick wooden worktable and watched, almost without blinking, as he sliced and chopped with skillful grace. She loved not only the taste and smell of such elegant dishes as salmon with black beans or moo shu pork with plum sauce but the look and feel of them as well. Years later Joyce Chen realized that Mandarin Chinese cuisine was a part of her life she simply could not give up.

In 1949 Joyce, her husband, Tom, and their two children, Helen and Stephen, lived in Shanghai. They, like thousands of others had fled northern China when the Japanese invaded during World War II. Now, years after the

Japanese defeat, Mao Zedong's Communist forces had again brought unrest and violence to mainland China. Millions of people, hoping to flee to Taiwan or Hong Kong or even farther west, had crowded into coastal cities. The Chens managed to get on board one of the last ships allowed to leave Shanghai for the United States.

The family eventually settled in Cambridge, Massachusetts, the home of Harvard University and the Massachusetts Institute of Technology. In her own kitchen Joyce tried to recreate the dishes she had known as a child. She made frequent shopping trips to Chinatown in nearby Boston to buy ingredients. She was disappointed, however, that none of the Chinese restaurants in Boston or Cambridge served the Mandarin dishes she loved. Instead they served Cantonese food, prepared in the style of the southern Chinese city of Canton (Guangzhou). Most Americans, Joyce soon learned, thought all Chinese food was alike and that the choices ranged from chop suey to chow mein, with little in between. So Joyce prepared her favorite dishes— Peking duck, hot-and-sour soup—at home. She often invited students from northern China who studied at the local universities to join the family for dinner.

In 1955 while her children attended school in Cambridge, Joyce prepared her favorite egg rolls and potstickers (fried dumplings) for the annual bake sale. Just after the sale began, Joyce arrived but she didn't see her food anywhere. She asked why the dishes had been removed. They were not removed, another mother answered; they sold out immediately. That was just the push Joyce needed to begin thinking about opening her own restaurant.

Three years later, in 1958, Joyce opened her first restaurant in Cambridge. It was in a largely Italian neighborhood, and so she renamed some of her favorite dishes. One of the most popular became Peking Ravioli, a pan-fried dumpling. Joyce Chen's restaurant soon attracted not only the famous and powerful from Harvard University but also blue-collar diners from Cambridge's other neighborhoods as well. Another of her regular customers was fellow Cambridge resident, Julia Child, who was well known for introducing classic French cuisine to Americans.

When professors and students from MIT complained that the restaurant's location was too close to Harvard, she opened a second one. A few years later there were three Joyce Chen restaurants in Cambridge. In the mid-1960s she compiled her favorite recipes into *The Joyce Chen Cookbook,* which became a best-seller. A few years later she became the host of *Joyce Chen Cooks,* a weekly TV show on PBS. In 1972 Joyce Chen and her son Stephen, a documentary filmmaker, went to China and made a film called *Joyce Chen's China,* which was also shown on public television.

By the late 1970s only one of Joyce Chen's dreams had not yet come true. She had not collaborated on a cookbook with her daughter Helen, who had also become a well-known chef. When Joyce Chen was diagnosed with Alzheimer's disease in the 1980s, the dream seemed over. Yet Helen wrote *Chinese Home Cooking,* based on her mother's recollections, as a tribute. The book was published in 1995, a year after Joyce Chen's death.

Helen Chen also took over Joyce Chen Inc., a cooking products business that her mother had founded. The company makes and distributes Eastern cookware, including woks, cutting boards, and knives for the American kitchen. Both Joyce and Helen Chen believed that, just as painters need the best brushes and musicians the finest instruments, cooks need the right tools to turn food into works of art.

An Wang

Computer Wizard
1920–1990

"Confidence," An Wang wrote in his autobiography, *Lessons*, "is sometimes rooted in the unpleasant, harsh aspects of life and not in warmth and safety."[14] His own childhood in China bears out this view. An Wang grew up during a time of war and political upheaval. Ahn was asked often to take on more responsibilities than other children his age. Yet his confidence in his own abilities never wavered. In fact his life's tragedies may have strengthened his resolve to succeed.

Born in Shanghai, China, An Wang was the oldest of five children. When he was six-years-old, his family moved to a city outside Shanghai where his father taught English in a private elementary school. Because this new school began with the third grade, An skipped first and second grades.

For the rest of his schooling in China, he was two years younger than his classmates.

At first schoolwork was difficult for Wang, but he soon managed to keep up with the older children. Throughout junior high and high school, he excelled in math and science but often needed extra help with other subjects. This was especially true when he entered one of the finest high schools in China. Several of his classes were taught in English and used university textbooks.

In 1936, at the age of sixteen, Wang entered Chiao Tung University, where he majored in electrical engineering and specialized in electronic communications. That same year his mother died, and then, in 1937, Japanese troops invaded China and occupied Shanghai. After Wang graduated in 1940, he remained at the university where he and eight former classmates secretly designed and built radios and transmitters for Chinese soldiers to use against the Japanese. Although weekly bombing raids interrupted their work, the team of engineers provided a valuable wartime service.

While working at the university, he received the news that his father had died. Now, as the war came to an end, there was little to keep him in China. When he was offered the opportunity to study American technology, he eagerly joined the two-year program.

Wang arrived in the United States in 1945. While waiting to be assigned to an American company, he began graduate studies at Harvard University. Four years later he received his doctoral degree in applied physics. While at Harvard, An Wang became a research assistant to Dr. Howard Aiken, a pioneer in computer development at the Harvard Computation Laboratory. Their work involved figuring out how to increase the speed at which a computer could store memory and read it. After much trial and error, Dr. Wang solved the problem by inventing magnetic "memory cores." The core memory system was used in most computers throughout the 1950s and 1960s, until it was replaced by silicon microchips.

In the early 1950s, Wang decided to patent his invention and start his own company—Wang Laboratories—to manufacture and sell his memory devices, which he called Deltamax cores. With only $600 in savings, he rented a tiny office in Boston and went to work. He started with a board of directors that included an attorney, one part-time assistant, and his wife, Lorraine.

By 1952 his work with digital counting devices began to pay off. His memory device had been installed in the scoreboard at New York's Shea Stadium and thus, for the first time, the public became aware of this marvelous invention. In 1955 An and Lorraine Wang became citizens of the United States and, shortly afterward, Wang Laboratories was incorporated. From then on, success seemed to follow success. Dr. Wang sold his patent for core memories to IBM in 1956. In 1964 his company came out with the first electronic scientific desk calculator—the forerunner of the desktop computer.

"People don't want technology, they want solutions to problems" was An Wang's simple philosophy, and it was perfect for the new electronic age. In the 1960s Wang Labs was the leading producer of electronic calculators; in the 1970s, word processors; and in the 1980s, office automation systems. He is credited with designing the first easy-to-use computer. And, because of his engineering genius and corporate vision, his company grew tenfold between 1977 and 1982. Wang Labs eventually took over a large area of the old mill town of Lowell, Massachusetts, where it employed thousands of people.

As the computer industry became more and more competitive, however, problems arose. After being in the lead for years, Wang Laboratories was suddenly overtaken by such established corporate giants as IBM, AT&T,

and Hewlett-Packard. In 1986 An Wang, whose health had been failing for several years, handed the reins of his company to his son, Frederick, and stepped down. Unfortunately even this move could not cure the ailing company. Frederick resigned as president in 1989. The following year Dr. An Wang died of throat cancer. In 1992 Wang Laboratories filed for protection under U.S. bankruptcy laws.

Even though his company no longer exists, time and circumstances cannot take away An Wang's extraordinary accomplishments. He surpassed his goal of providing workers with the equipment and services that would make their jobs easier. He also gave back to his community and society, donating millions of dollars to hospitals, homeless shelters, art organizations, and projects in Boston's Chinatown.

Sammy Lee

Doctor, Olympic Diver, Coach
1920–

"Work hard in America," Sammy Lee's parents told him, "and you can gain much in life." That's just what their son did. In 1947 he graduated from medical school. A year later he won the Summer Olympics championship in platform diving in London, England. Four years later in Helsinki, Finland, he became the first person to win back-to-back Olympic gold medals in diving.

Born in Fresno, California, in 1920, Sammy Lee was surrounded by a family who loved him. The outside world, however, was not nearly as warm and caring. In the farming communities of California, Korean Americans were victims of cruel racial discrimination. Thinking the Lees were Japanese, many whites taunted them with racial slurs. This was doubly insulting because the Japanese, who were illegally occupying Korea at the time, were enemies of Koreans. But the Lees did not protest the discrimination. Mr. Lee believed that the surest way of fighting back was to change others' false opinions by working hard to prove them wrong.

Sammy Lee followed his father's advice. He set two goals for himself and decided not to let anything stand in the way of achieving them: he wanted to become a doctor and the world's best diver. When his friends said that his goals were unobtainable, he replied that they obviously did not know the real Sammy Lee.

As World War II raged, Lee graduated from Occidental College and then joined the United States Army Medical Corps in 1942. Following the war, he enrolled at the University of Southern California Medical School, all the while maintaining a rigorous diving schedule. In 1948, a year after graduating, he earned a place on the U.S. Olympic team.

At the Olympic Games in London, England, Lee achieved one of the two goals he had set for himself. He proved that he was the world's best high diver. (Today "high diving" is called "platform diving.") In 1952, after marrying and beginning his medical career, Lee achieved his second goal in life—he became a doctor. As if this was not enough, Lee did it again! While competing at the Olympics in Helsinki, Finland, he won a second gold medal, making him the second Asian Pacific American to win two gold medals in Olympic diving competitions.

As impressive as his Olympic medals were, Lee's career since then has been just as remarkable. Dr. Lee has managed to combine his two loves— he is a respected ear, nose, and throat specialist, and he coaches promising young divers. In 1956 he was President Dwight Eisenhower's representative at the Melbourne Olympics, a position he also filled in 1976 and 1988 under different presidential administrations. Then in 1958 he became the first non-white to win the James E. Sullivan award for outstanding achievement in sports.

During the 1970s and 1980s Lee helped guide Greg Louganis to his two stunning Olympic diving victories. (Louganis's story is told later in the book.) In 1984 Lee was an Olympic flag bearer and torch runner at the Los Angeles Summer Games. In 1990 he was elected to the U.S. Olympic Hall of Fame as a genuine symbol of the best Olympic spirit.

True to the beliefs of his father, Sammy Lee worked hard and gained much in life. His achievements proved skeptics wrong and changed the opinions of many prejudiced people.

Yoshiko Uchida

Children's Author
1921–1992

In her book *The Birthday Visitor,* Yoshiko Uchida tells of a seven-year-old girl named Emi Watanabe who is growing up between two very different cultures in Berkeley, California, during the 1920s. To create a character like Emi, who loves nothing more than visiting her neighbor, "Grandfather" Wada, and his lovely Japanese garden, Yoshiko Uchida drew on her own experiences. Her parents had both come to America from Japan, and the family had settled in the heart of Berkeley's Japanese community. As a child, Yoshiko Uchida knew many people like Mr. Wada, whom she loved dearly, but who also seemed more a part of the past than the future. Uchida, like many other second-generation Americans (Nisei), struggled constantly to find her own way between her family's heritage and the new world. How was it possible to be part of both cultures?

After Japan attacked the United States naval base at Pearl Harbor on December 7, 1941, and America entered World War II, hatred, fear, and suspicion of all Japanese Americans escalated. Many found themselves in the difficult position of having to renounce their ancestral homeland to prove their loyalty to the United States. By February 1942, Executive Order 9066 proscribed areas from which "any or all persons may be excluded." Although the word "Japanese" was not used, the order was directed solely at people of Japanese ancestry. It set in motion the forced removal of 120,000 Japanese Americans, the majority of whom were American citizens, from their homes and places of business. Although no evidence of disloyalty or sabotage could be found, they were imprisoned in poorly equipped and isolated camps under the guise of "military necessity."

Yoshiko Uchida had been studying for final exams at the University of California library on December 7, 1941. When she returned home, she learned that her father had been taken off by the FBI. After questioning, Mr. Uchida was taken to a prisoner-of-war camp in Montana. His wife and two daughters, however, did not know where he was until a year later when the family was reunited at a relocation camp in Topaz, Utah.

At Topaz, Uchida became a teacher at one of the makeshift schools the Japanese quickly established to continue their children's educations. Of her terrible years in the hot Utah desert, Yoshiko Uchida mostly remembered the dust, which swirled around the camp and poured into every crack in the barracks. During one of the frequent dust storms, she wrote: "[t]he wind reached such force we thought our barrack would be torn from its feeble foundations. Pebbles and rocks rained against the walls. . . . The air was so thick with the smoke-like dust, my mouth was gritty with it and my lungs seemed penetrated by it. For hours the wind shrieked around our shuddering barrack."[15]

In 1943 Yoshiko Uchida was able to leave Topaz to attend graduate school at Smith College in Massachusetts. She left the camp neither depressed nor discouraged but determined to prove that Americans were wrong about the Japanese. "I felt a tremendous sense of responsibility to make good, not just for myself, but for all Japanese Americans. . . . It was sometimes an awesome burden to bear."[16]

When the war ended, Yoshiko's parents were finally able to leave Topaz. Several years later they purchased a house just two blocks from the one they were forced to leave during the war. Their daughter, after receiving a fellowship to study in Japan for two years, traveled throughout the countryside, collecting folktales for her writing. She returned to the United States with a renewed sense of pride in her Japanese heritage.

With this new confidence and self-knowledge, she began writing books for young people. In all, Yoshiko Uchida wrote twenty-eight books. In *The Birthday Visitor, Jar of Dreams, The Best Bad Thing, The Happiest Ending*, and *Samurai of Gold Hill*, among others, she created stories and characters based on her own past. She described her wartime experiences in *Journey to Topaz* and *Journey Home* and in the nonfiction book for adults, *Desert Exile*. Her writing brings important knowledge to all Americans. Her message was that hope and pride are possible even during the darkest years of discrimination, persecution, and imprisonment.

Jade Snow Wong

Author, Ceramicist
1922–

"Respect and order," writes Jade Snow Wong in her book *Fifth Chinese Daughter* about growing up in San Francisco's Chinatown during the 1920s and 1930s, were the most important concepts of life. The authority of Wong's parents, who had immigrated from China to San Francisco at the turn of the century, was never questioned. You must always, they told her many times, do the proper thing and, especially, show respect for your elders.

"Respect" demanded that Jade Snow Wong never even call her older brother and sisters by their given names—Blessing from Heaven, Jade Swallow, or Jade Lotus. Instead she had to say, "Older Brother, would you mind if I. . ." or "Fourth Older Sister, if it pleases you. . ." And then she waited for the answers, never interrupting, never challenging.

The family lived in the back of a small garment factory owned by Mr. Wong. Family life and work were closely linked since the Wong's kitchen and dining room were on the same floor as the factory's sewing room. After her mother prepared the family's breakfast each morning, she walked down the hall and took her place at a sewing table along with the other employees. Most of the women workers brought their small children along with them and often prepared their own meals in the Wong's kitchen.

When Jade Snow Wong was old enough to begin first grade at the nearby American school, her father continued—as he had for several years—to tutor her early each morning in Chinese history, literature, and calligraphy. When she turned eight, her father enrolled her at a Chinese school. This meant that each day after Wong left her American school, she walked through Chinatown to another school, where she received a proper Chinese education. She did not return home until after eight in the evening.

Jade Snow Wong was proud that her father considered her a bright student. But she was sorry that her many hours in school left her no time to play with her younger sister, Jade Precious Stone, or her baby brother. However, as with every decision made by her parents, her opinion was of no importance.

Still, there was at least some family fun each week. After their long days of studying and chores, the Wong children looked forward to Saturday nights, when Mama took them to the neighborhood movie theater. There they watched cowboys and Indians, runaway stagecoaches, and even Tarzan. When they arrived home from the movies, the Sunday paper would have been delivered, and the children read the comics.

Sunday was a more serious time. The family again rose early and, after reading their Chinese Bible, attended a nearby Chinese Christian church. After lunch Mama and the children set off on a walk together, winding their way through Chinatown's colorful streets. "Next to the Saturday movies," Jade Wong remembered, "these Sunday walks were the best part of the week."

As Jade Snow Wong neared the end of high school and began to think about college, she questioned more and more the strict discipline imposed on her by her parents. She wanted to attend college but knew that, since her parents believed higher education was not proper for girls, she would have to pay the cost herself. While still in high school, she became a housekeeper for a wealthy white American family and eventually saved up enough money to put herself through junior college.

After two years Jade Snow won a scholarship to Mills College. Surrounded by privileged white Americans, she thought hard about her Chinese upbringing. Why, she wondered, did my parents prepare me to be a good Chinese daughter when I live in the United States? Why did they teach me to be silent and obedient, when Americans succeed by thinking for themselves?

Fifth Chinese Daughter, written when Jade Snow Wong was still in her twenties, grapples with these questions. "The new world was full of light and promised independence," she wrote, "but the path between the two worlds was . . . a rough one."[7] As a second-generation Chinese American, she walked that path, searching for an identity that would allow her to be respected as both Chinese and American.

After the publication of *Fifth Chinese Daughter* in 1945, Jade Snow Wong traveled widely throughout the United States and Asia. Her book became a best-seller. Yet when she returned to her parents' home in San Francisco, they would not mention *Fifth Chinese Daughter*.

Since 1950 Jade Snow Wong has lived quietly in San Francisco, working as a writer and lecturer but mostly as a ceramicist. She has become a master of this ancient Chinese art, using hand-carved bamboo to decorate her vases. Ceramics, it seems, has helped this Chinese American find her own path between the old world and the new.

Daniel K. Inouye

U.S. Senator
1924–

"Respectable poverty," is how Daniel Inouye describes his family's status during his childhood years in Honolulu, Hawaii. His father, Hyotaro, and his grandparents had come to the Hawaiian Islands from Japan in the 1880s after a fire in the Inouye home left the entire family destitute. By working on the islands' sugar planta-tions, Daniel Inouye's grandfather had hoped to earn enough in three years to pay off his family's debts and then return to Japan.

By the time the debts were paid, Hyotaro Inouye had decided to stay in Hawaii. He married a Japanese woman in 1923 and a year later their son Daniel was born. Daniel attended both an American public school and a Japanese language school. He graduated from high school and entered the

University of Hawaii in 1942. But college, at least the first time around, lasted only one year. In 1943, two years after the United States went to war with Japan, Daniel Inouye enlisted in the U.S. Army. He served in the all-Nisei (a Japanese word meaning "children of Japanese immigrants") 442nd Regimental Combat Team.

This regiment was formed in 1942 after young Japanese American men, ashamed of Japan's attack on Pearl Harbor, asked Congress to let them show their loyalty to the United States. Just as thousands of Japanese Americans were being moved to relocation camps—often referred to as America's concentration camps—throughout the West, the 442nd headed for Europe's front lines. Composed entirely of volunteers, this became the most decorated army unit in U.S. history.

In 1944 Daniel Inouye distinguished himself as a platoon leader in Italy's Po Valley. Just before the European war ended, he led an assault on a heavily defended German infantry position. Even though his right arm had been shattered by a grenade and he'd been shot in the stomach and legs, Inouye managed to throw a grenade into each of three German machine-gun nests, saving the lives of his entire unit. For his bravery he received the Distinguished Service Cross (upgraded to a Medal of Honor in 2000), the Bronze Star, and the Purple Heart. He also lost his right arm and spent almost two years in an army hospital.

Back in Hawaii in the late 1940s, he finished his bachelor's degree at the university and then headed to the mainland to attend law school at George Washington University. While in Washington, D.C., he volunteered for the Democratic National Committee and was bitten by the political "bug." He decided to pursue his own career in politics and so, when he returned to Hawaii in 1952, he set out building a strong Democratic Party in the territory. When Hawaii became a state in 1959, Daniel K. Inouye became its first congressman in the U.S. House of Representatives.

Within a few years he was elected to the U.S. Senate—the first Asian American in such a high position—and he rose quickly to positions of leadership. Highlights of his thirty-year Senate career include serving on the Senate Watergate Committee, which was set up in the early 1970s to investigate charges of illegal activities by officials of the administration of President Richard M. Nixon. His patient but determined questioning impressed the huge national television audience. He has since chaired other important Senate committees and in the mid-1980s was again in the public limelight as he served on the Senate Select Committee investigating the Iran-Contra affair.

Today Senator Inouye and his wife of over fifty years, the former Margaret Shinobu Awamura, divide their time between Washington, D.C., and Honolulu.

Tsung Dao Lee

1926–

Chen Ning Yang

1922–
Winners, Nobel Prize for Physics

Tsung Dao Lee

Most afternoons the two physicists would go to their favorite Chinese restaurant near the Columbia University campus. There they would enjoy a multicourse meal and then drink tea into the afternoon. Over cup after cup they would talk animatedly about new ideas in physics. Speaking in Mandarin Chinese, their voices would become very loud and then very soft, and their hands never stayed still. Many in the restaurant thought the two men were arguing when, in fact, they were simply thinking out loud, bouncing ideas off each other, just as they had been doing since they were both students at the University of Chicago.

Chen Ning Yang

It was after one such lunch in May 1956 that the Drs. Lee and Yang decided to begin the experiments that would challenge one of the most basic principles of physics, the conservation of parity law. This law states that elementary particles in nature are always symmetrical. In other words, there is no way of telling which of a set of actions is real and which is the mirror image or—to put it another way—which side is left and which is right. For their work in overturning this fundamental law, they were given the 1957 Nobel Prize for Physics.

Tsung Dao Lee was born in Shanghai, China, the son of a businessman. Chen Ning Yang was born in far northern China but raised and educated in Beijing. His father, a university professor and well-known mathematician, encouraged his son to study the physical sciences.

The two first met at the National Southwest Associated University in Kunming, China, where they had both come after fleeing Japanese invaders. In 1945 Chen Ning Yang received a full scholarship to the University of Chicago. A year later Tsung Dao Lee followed and stayed until 1950, when he received the Ph.D. degree. Dr. Yang left Chicago in 1949 and resettled at Princeton University's Institute for Advanced Study.

Drs. Lee and Yang were reunited in 1953 when Dr. Lee accepted a position at New York City's Columbia University, not too far from Princeton, New Jersey. The two began an intense period of teamwork, exchanging ideas over the phone, in the lab, and, of course, at their favorite Chinese restaurant. Inside the comfortable dining room they challenged each other with daring new ideas.

When they decided to undertake their test of the conservation of parity law, they chose a fellow Chinese physicist, Dr. Chien-Shiung Wu, to perform the experiments. Madame Wu, as she was usually called, was a senior Columbia faculty member and often joined the two for lunch. (Her story was given earlier.)

Six months after the start of Madame Wu's complicated experiments, she was able to tell Drs. Lee and Yang that her results proved their theory. They announced their findings to a stunned scientific community early in 1957. On January 15 of that year, the *New York Times* described the news as "the most important development in physics in the past ten years. . . . The fruits of the new discovery may not ripen for another quarter century or more, but scientists are now confident that they are at last on the right road to a better understanding of the forces that govern our universe."

The impact of their theory was such that that very year, 1957, Drs. Lee and Yang were awarded the Nobel Prize. After earning this most distinguished prize in science, the two settled into long, successful academic careers. Dr. Yang continued at Princeton's Institute for Advanced Study until 1965 when he became the director of the Institute for Theoretical Physics at the State University of New York at Stony Brook. Dr. Lee has been the Enrico Fermi Professor of Physics at Columbia University since 1964.

Patsy Takemoto Mink

Member, U.S. House of Representatives
1927–2002

She has been called the most important woman in Hawaiian politics since Queen Liliuokalani. Patsy Mink was first elected to Congress in 1964 and worked hard for Hawaii ever since, fighting for civil rights and equal opportunity. "What I bring to Congress," she once said, "is a Hawaiian background of tolerance and equality that can contribute a great deal to better understanding between races."

Patsy Takemoto was born in 1927 on the Hawaiian island of Maui. As a little girl, she remembers listening to what were called President Franklin

Delano Roosevelt's "fireside chats" on the radio and being very moved by his words. The president's informal talks with the nation showed Patsy that "possibly the highest achievement is to find a place in life that permits one to be of service to his fellow men."

The teenager's career in public service began early. She was president of the student body at Maui High School and valedictorian of the senior class. After graduating from the University of Hawaii, Honolulu, in 1948, she enrolled at the University of Chicago Law School. There she met John Mink, whom she married in 1951. After her graduation from the University of Chicago in 1953, the Minks settled in Hawaii.

Patsy Mink went into private law practice in Honolulu. She also began dabbling in politics, first as founder of the Oahu Young Democrats and then as the Hawaiian delegate to the Young Democratic National Convention. Her first elected position was to the Hawaiian house of representatives in 1957 and then to the Hawaiian senate, first in 1959 and again in 1963, after the territory had become a state.

In 1964 Patsy Mink ran for Congress the old-fashioned way: her husband, John, was her volunteer campaign manager, and friends and coworkers offered their free services. With only a tiny campaign budget, she easily beat her Republican challenger.

Once in the nation's capital she wasted no time getting much-needed legislation passed for the construction of schools in U.S. Pacific territories and for education and child-welfare programs. An ardent foe of the Vietnam War, Patsy Mink gave many impassioned speeches on the floor of the House Chamber. The war was not only unjust, she told her fellow members, it ate up huge amounts of money that could have been used better for social programs to improve the lives of the neediest Americans.

In 1977 Patsy Mink retired from the House. She and John and their daughter, Gwendolyn, returned to Honolulu. Patsy resumed her law practice and began to lecture at the University of Hawaii. She seemed content with her quieter life.

In 1990, however, following the death of Senator Spark Matsunaga and a shuffling of Hawaii's congressional delegation, Patsy Mink accepted a seat in the House of Representatives. She headed to Washington, ready once again to serve Hawaii and its unique multiracial population. She was reelected for still another term in November 2000 and continued her work as a leader in women's issues in general and as an advocate of family and medical leave, workplace fairness, and universal health care. In September 2002 Patsy Mink won the Democratic primary election for her seat in the U.S. House of Representatives. She was considered an almost certain winner in the November election. Yet on September 28, Patsy died in a Honolulu hospital from viral pneumonia, a complication from chicken pox. She was seventy-four-years-old.

K.W. Lee

Investigative Reporter
1928–

"Few ethnic minorities have been so devastated in such a single blow since World War II, singled out for destruction as the newest scapegoat for all the ills—imagined or real—of the murderous inner cities of our country."

—K.W. Lee, October 1992, after receiving a humanitarian award from the city of Los Angeles for his work in mediating between the Korean and African American communities during the riots of April 1992

That K.W. Lee was born to be an investigative reporter has probably never been questioned. No one, however, could have predicted the far-reaching scope and influence of his "beat." From Seoul, Korea, to West Virginia coal country to the mean streets of Los Angeles, K.W. Lee has always been ready to ask questions, listen to the answers and when needed, help fellow members of the human community.

Born in Kaesong, Korea, K.W. Lee studied English literature at Korea University, Seoul, before accepting a scholarship to West Virginia University.

Shortly after arriving in the United States in 1950, war broke out in his homeland, and he, like many of his countrymen, decided that returning to Korea was too dangerous. After earning his bachelor of science degree in journalism from West Virginia, he entered the University of Illinois, where he earned a master's degree in 1955.

The next year he returned to Appalachia to begin his newspaper career. After a short stint with Tennessee's *Kingsport Times and News,* he accepted a job with West Virginia's *Charleston Gazette.* At the time, Mr. Lee recalled, "the editor of the Gazette needed a black reporter. For some reason he chose me."

Being the paper's only minority reporter gave Lee a window on some of the century's most important events. In the late 1950s he covered the civil rights movement, following Martin Luther King Jr. as he traveled throughout the South. Lee also covered the hard-fought legislative battles that would eventually bring help to victims of the deadly black lung disease in Appalachia. Black lung, a chronic disease caused by inhaling coal dust, afflicted thousands of Appalachian coal miners, leaving them and their families destitute. Laws passed in the early 1960s offered protection and compensation to the miners.

After spending the entire decade of the 1960s at the *Charleston Gazette,* K.W. Lee moved his West Virginia–born wife and children to Sacramento, California, where he was finally able to put his well-honed journalistic skills to work serving the Asian, especially Korean, community. As he walked the streets of Koreatown, he listened to his ethnic compatriots. Then he did something few other reporters of his race or language had done before: He explained their concerns and needs to a wide English-speaking readership.

For his tireless work, he received numerous major journalistic awards, including several for outstanding community service. In 1979, after writing a series of investigative articles detailing the events surrounding the wrongful murder conviction of a young Korean immigrant named Chol Soo Lee, Lee received awards from both the Associated Press's News Executives Council and Columbia University.

In 1979 K.W. Lee became the editor and publisher of the *Koreatown Weekly*. Later he was named the editor of the English edition of the *Korea Times*. His familiarity with California's large cities plus his dedicated social activism made him uniquely qualified, therefore, to become the mediator between the Korean and African American communities after 1992s devastating riots in Los Angeles. He called 1992 a year of "economic holocaust" for nearly a quarter million Korean immigrants in the Los Angeles area.

K.W. Lee's faith in the possibility of new beginnings was strengthened when, later that year, he underwent a successful liver transplant operation. "My new liver," he wrote shortly afterward, "may have belonged to an African American or a Latino or Anglo. What does it matter? We are all entangled in an unbroken human chain of interdependence and mutual survival."

Gerald Tsai Jr.

Financier
1928–

"The hottest money manager on Wall Street" and the "complete dealster" are two ways people describe Gerald Tsai Jr. Attention to the wheelings and dealings of this first-generation Chinese American has been intense ever since he burst onto the scene in the mid-1960s. Today, more than thirty-five years later, his reputation in the financial world is nothing short of legendary.

Gerry, as he is commonly known, was born to a wealthy Shanghai family in 1928. His father, a textile industrialist, had graduated from the University of Michigan in the United States. Just after World War II the Tsai family was forced by political events to escape from Shanghai. Gerry Tsai was eighteen when he came to Boston and enrolled as a student of economics at Boston University.

After receiving both bachelor's and master's degrees, Tsai went to work for Fidelity Fund, a Boston investment firm. He gained a reputation as a hard worker and began excelling in judging stock deals with amazing accuracy. In fact he became so successful at managing money that by the mid-1960s, people were watching his movements before making their own decisions about buying and selling stock. News that Gerry Tsai was about to buy or sell a block of stock could force its value either up or down.

Tsai made Wall Street history in February 1966 when, by virtue of his reputation, he convinced 150,000 investors to buy 42 million shares in his new Manhattan Fund. As founder and president of the fund, his assets were valued at $270 million.

Asked at the time how he managed to overcome racial and national prejudice to become the most successful manager on Wall Street, he replied simply, "I encountered no barriers." He went on to explain that if he buys a share of American Motors for an investor at $100 and sells it at a profit of $50, does it matter if his skin is white or yellow? Observers point out that his self-confidence is born of hard work and conviction. Gerry Tsai simply does his homework better than anyone else. When he decides to buy or sell large blocks of stock, he knows that, based on all the available information, he is making the right decision.

Shortly after beginning the Manhattan Fund, Tsai sold it to CNA, which is a large insurance company. In the process he virtually took control of CNA. Later, after more buying and selling—always perfectly timed—he gained controlling interest in the huge American Can Company.

In 1986, twenty years after the start of the Manhattan Fund, Gerry Tsai pulled off his biggest success yet. As chief executive officer of American Can, he began to sell off parts of that company until, one day, American Can became Primerica, a financial services company. Two years later the deal master sold Primerica for $1.5 billion.

Now in his seventies, Gerald Tsai Jr. is chairman and president of Tsai Management. Many wonder if Gerry Tsai will ever truly retire and enjoy one of the lovely homes he has built for himself. He has almost left the financial scene before but, lured by the opportunity to make huge profits, has always returned. Perhaps, as one writer noted, the hardest task facing Gerald Tsai is both filling his own shoes and fulfilling his own legend.

Toshiko Akiyoshi

Jazz Pianist, Composer, Band Leader
1929–

"Against all odds" could be the tag line for Toshiko Akiyoshi's career in jazz music. Who would have thought a Japanese woman could excel in a uniquely American art form that has deep African roots? She herself admits making unlikely choices in her music, but as she once told an interviewer, she found such deep feeling and certainty in jazz, she could not *not* play it.

While living as a child in Manchuria, China, in the 1930s, Toshiko Akiyoshi studied classical piano. She did not learn about jazz until her family returned to Japan following the war in 1947. Then this petite, determined young woman became interested in the music that was introduced by American soldiers after World War II. When some American jazz artists visited Japan in the mid-1950s, they recognized her talent and convinced her to move to the United States where she could get more training.

Toshiko Akiyoshi studied at the Berklee School of Music in Boston from 1956 to 1959. She credits Berklee with helping her to organize her ideas about music and to understand why some compositions work while others do not. After graduating she hit the club circuit and became a highly regarded pianist, specializing in bebop. She toured with Charles Mingus and Charlie Mariano, whom she married in 1961. The newlyweds moved to Japan, where they lived for four years before returning to New York City.

During the 1960s Toshiko Akiyoshi grew into a superb jazz instrumentalist, arranger, and teacher. She played at jazz festivals around the world, including the Newport Jazz Festival and Japan's World Jazz Festival. In 1971 she played at New York's Carnegie Hall with Lew Tabackin, a saxophonist and flutist who had become her second husband.

Toshiko Akiyoshi and Lew Tabackin moved to Los Angles, where they put together a sixteen-piece band, the Akiyoshi-Tabackin Big Band. The Big Band followed in the tradition of the renown conductor and composer Duke Ellington, who allowed each musician's unique sound to be part of the orchestra's identity. Their album *Kogun*, recorded in Japan in 1974, won several prestigious music awards. The band went on to record several more albums and to establish itself as the leading big band in jazz. For many years they have topped *Downbeat* magazine's "Best Band" critics poll. Akiyoshi's own work has won her fourteen Grammy nominations.

The band, which became known as Toshiko Akiyoshi's Jazz Orchestra featuring Lew Tabackin, allowed its leader to expand her talents as a composer. She often added elements of Japanese music to her scores, giving them a striking richness. The best-selling *Kogun*, for example, was inspired by the real-life story of a Japanese soldier who was found hiding in a Philippine jungle thirty years after the end of World War II.

Throughout the 1970s and 1980s, Toshiko Akiyoshi continued to expand her talents as a pianist. She has given several piano concerts at New York's Carnegie Hall. In 1984 this bold and tenacious woman was the subject of a documentary film called *Toshiko Akiyoshi: Jazz Is My Native Language.*

Toshiko Akiyoshi's contributions to the world of jazz are unique. As a pianist, composer, arranger, and conductor, she has used her Japanese roots to flavor her music. Still, she is quick to add, her musical philosophy can be summed up by one of Duke Ellington's song lyrics: "It don't mean a thing if you ain't got that swing."

Chang-Lin Tien

University Chancellor
1935–

When Chang-Lin Tien arrived in Kentucky from Taiwan to attend the University of Louisville, he had already lived through the Japanese occupation of his Chinese homeland and his family's escape from the Communists in 1949. "I was a refugee," he remembered. He felt pursuing graduate studies in the United States would be a quiet break from Asia's nearly constant political turmoil.

But it was 1956 and Chang-Lin Tien faced something new in Kentucky: racial discrimination. Throughout the South, drinking fountains, public restrooms, and lunch counters were marked with signs that read either "White" or "Colored." Since Asians were rare in Kentucky at the time, no one seemed to agree which category Tien fit into. Sometimes he was told to stand or sit with whites, other times he was roughly ordered toward the sign marked "Colored only."

Just a few years later, as a young faculty member at the University of California at Berkeley, he found that affordable apartments were off limits to "Orientals." When, in 1990, Professor Tien was made the chancellor, or head, of University of California at Berkeley (and its 31,000 students), the number of minorities in America had grown and their civil rights were better protected. Since he was the first Asian American to lead a major research university, he himself was a symbol of this progress. Yet Chang-Lin Tien always reminded students and faculty alike that the university would only achieve greatness by celebrating, rather than ignoring, cultural differences. "Excellence through diversity" was the phrase the new chancellor repeated again and again.

Chang-Lin Tien was born in Wuhan, China, to a wealthy banking family. During World War II the Tien family fled the occupying Japanese army and took refuge in Shanghai. They escaped to Taiwan when the Communists, led by Mao Zedong, came to power. In Taiwan's capital, Taipei, Tien's father was given a high position in the government of Chiang Kai-shek, and the family prospered once again. When Mr. Tien died suddenly in 1952, the family was pushed toward poverty.

In 1956 the twenty-one-year-old engineering student borrowed $3,000 in order to complete graduate studies in the United States. He stayed in Louisville long enough to receive his master's degree, and then he enrolled at Princeton University in New Jersey. There he received his doctoral degree in electrical engineering in 1959. When, during that same year, Tien was offered a teaching position at the Berkeley campus, he flew back to Taiwan and married his high-school sweetheart. The newlyweds set off for a new life in California.

Chang-Lin Tien did not let Berkeley's tense racial climate stop his climb to success. He eventually became the head of the mechanical engineering department and vice-chancellor of research. As civil rights laws were passed in Washington, D.C., and in state governments throughout the country, institutions like the University of California became more tolerant as well.

Yet there were still problems. During times of economic hardship or political uncertainty, minorities often find themselves targets of criticism. When Chang-Lin Tien became chancellor in 1990, the governor of California, Pete Wilson, often blamed state budget problems on minorities. They needed expensive state services, the governor said, but did not pay enough in taxes to make up the difference. These accusations may have been unfounded, but when repeated by political leaders, many average citizens believed they were true. In a state like California, where the number of non-whites equals the number of whites, this can make for very uncomfortable race relations.

Not surprisingly the chancellor's job was often a difficult balancing act. One of the chancellor's responsibilities was to raise money for the institution so that tuition could be kept as low as possible. Chang-Lin Tien, who still speaks English with a heavy Mandarin Chinese accent, turned to Asia. Asian government and business leaders were full of pride that one of their own was the leader of a great American university. When Chancellor Tien made his frequent trips to Asia, he was also greeted by the University of California's active alumni groups in the region.

The chancellor cannot, of course, act on behalf of only one minority group. When in 1990 he allowed the California football team to play a bowl game in Arizona—which at the time did not honor Martin Luther King Day—African American organizations complained loudly. Chancellor Tien, known as a polite listener, had to admit he had a lot to learn about the political side of his job. As one observer noted, the task of "redefining America" was bound to have its challenges.

Chang-Lin Tien stepped down as the University of California's chancellor in 1997 and is today University Professor Emeritus of Mechanical Engineering.

Norman Mineta

U.S. Congressman, Secretary of Commerce, Secretary of Transportation 1932–

In February 1943 President Franklin Roosevelt signed an executive order that called 120,000 American citizens of Japanese descent "subversive" and sent them to remote concentration camps. "I was 10 years old and wearing my Cub Scout uniform," Norman Mineta remembered, "when we were packed onto a train in San Jose."[18] When they arrived at Heart Mountain, Wyoming, they found their new "home" surrounded by prison wire and guarded by soldiers holding machine guns.

As bitter as this experience was for Norman Mineta and his family, it left him eager for a life in public service. When World War II was over, the Mineta family returned to San Jose, California. Norman Mineta attended the University of California at Berkeley, graduating in 1953. He served in the U.S. Army for three years and then helped run his father's San Jose insurance business. Since Japanese families had lost so much during their internment in the 1940s, all family members felt it their duty to help each other reestablish businesses and resettle lives.

Though Mineta was interested in politics, he did not run for office until 1967. That year he became the first nonwhite city-council member in San Jose. Then in 1971 he was elected mayor, becoming the first Asian American to lead a major American city. Four years later he was elected to the U.S. House of Representatives and served for the next twenty years, retiring in 1995.

For Norman Mineta "retirement" meant taking a position as a top executive at Lockheed-Martin, the huge aerospace and defense company. After years on the House Transportation Committee, he was very familiar with issues of importance to the industry. Norman Mineta had also championed legislation important to the computer industry, which was not surprising since his congressional district included Silicon Valley, home of many prominent high-tech companies.

When President Bill Clinton picked the former Congressman to become Secretary of Commerce, another "first" was added to Norman Mineta's long list—this time he became the first Asian American to serve on a president's cabinet. When President George W. Bush began to form his cabinet in early 2001, he asked Norman Mineta to serve in his administration as Secretary of Transportation. Since Secretary Mineta is a Democrat, he was flattered to be offered such an important position by a Republican president.

The year 2001 became an important one for the country's Secretary of Transportation. After terrorists hijacked four planes on September 11 and used them to kill thousands of people in New York City, Washington, D.C., and Pennsylvania, the department was in the spotlight. The secretary's leadership has been particularly important in helping Americans regain confidence in the airline industry, as well as in other forms of transportation.

Still, despite his familiarity with the fields of transportation and high technology, Norman Mineta is most proud of his achievements in civil rights. He helped pass the Civil Liberties Act of 1988, which issued an official apology and $20,000 for each living inmate of the Japanese internment camps. For his courageous efforts in the field of civil rights, Norman Mineta was awarded the Martin Luther King Jr. Commemorative Medal.

Nam June Paik

Video Artist, Composer
1932–

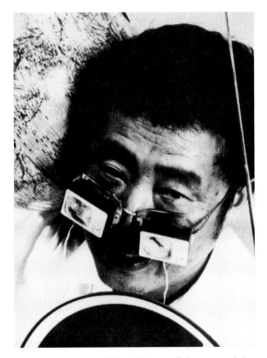

Although Nam June Paik is a serious musical composer and visual artist, he does not object if audiences greet his work with laughter. His "action concerts" of the 1960s, where he smashed pianos and poured shampoo on audience members were either loved or hated. Back then, Paik would just shrug when asked about the reaction. "Being from a poor country like Korea," he would say with a mischievous smile, "I have an obligation to be entertaining."

This "obligation" led him from bizarre performance pieces to the world of television technology and video art. He claimed fame as the first person to alter the electromagnetic field of the cathode ray tube (CRT) for art's sake. After years as an avant-garde musician specializing in electronic music, it was not surprising, given his wit and daring, that he would use TV technology to produce art. His contributions have earned him international acclaim and major exhibits at the world's major museums.

Born in Seoul, Korea, he was the youngest of five children of a wealthy factory owner. In 1950 Paik and his family left war-torn Korea as refugees and went first to Hong Kong and then to Tokyo. Paik hid his interest in music from his parents, who felt such a career was unworthy of their son. When he enrolled at the University of Tokyo, he studied philosophy and dabbled in music on the side.

His father happily sent him to graduate school in Germany, where Paik intended to work on a doctoral degree. He studied at the Universities of Munich and Cologne, but he gradually began to devote himself exclusively to music. Encouraged by one teacher in Cologne, he joined a group of experimental composers. In 1958 the American composer John Cage visited Germany, and Nam June Paik's life was changed forever.

At the time John Cage was interested in making music that was theatrical. Nam June Paik loved that Cage was willing to look foolish and make the audience laugh in order to move his music in new directions. Then, just as Paik's "action concerts" were the subject of awe and outrage, he switched his attention to video technology.

He began taking apart black and white TV sets and hooking them up to microphones. The sound waves then made the TV images leap across the screen. He reversed the black and white controls to make negative images and then interfered with the electromagnetic field to produce bizarre shapes. He held his first video art show in Germany in 1963.

Later he began experimenting with color sets and invented the concept of "video painting." Accompanied by a robot on his first visit to the United States in 1964, Paik soon settled in New York City. There, in 1965, he showed his altered television sets to enthusiastic audiences.

The first showing of Paik's video art on home television came in 1968 when a public television station asked him to produce an hour-long special called "The Medium Is the Medium." That program's success spurred another, which featured a video synthesizer that Paik had designed and built himself. This machine received audio and video input from many sources. In "Video Commune," people on the street were invited either to have their forms turned into televised images or to play with the set's console controls.

For the next thirty years Paik took video technology and turned it into both art and entertainment. That he is a serious artist was confirmed in 1982 when the Whitney Museum of American Art honored him with a retrospective that featured sixty video installations, sculptures, and musical scores. The show then traveled to Chicago, San Francisco, Berlin, and Vienna.

A U.S. citizen since 1976, today Nam June Paik lives in New York City with his Japanese wife, who is also a video artist. In the summer of 2000, New York's Guggenheim Museum held a major retrospective of Nam June Paik's work.

Yoko Ono

Artist, Musician
1933–

In the 1960s Yoko Ono was part of New York City's avant-garde art scene and best known for what she called her "instructional pieces." One of these was named *Painting to Be Stepped On,* and it consisted of an empty canvas on a gallery floor. Those who entered the room were asked to step on the canvas and, in that way, to create their own art. Another was called simply *Cut Piece.* During these performances viewers were invited on stage to cut away at Ono's clothes. Though she considered herself a serious artist, Yoko Ono never cared about creating beautiful objects. Instead she liked to inspire certain feelings, which she then believed became works of art in themselves.

Yoko Ono was used to having people make fun of her art. When, in 1966, John Lennon of the Beatles came to an opening of her work at a

London gallery, he was ready for a laugh. He walked through the doors, looked around briefly, and then walked toward an exhibit called simply *Apple*. He lifted the green apple from its glass plinth and took a big bite. Even the hard-to-shock Yoko was startled. "Oh, I was terribly cross!" she remembered. But she had to admit it was pretty funny.

Before long a romance blossomed between John and Yoko. They appeared everywhere together and even formed a new rock band, the Plastic Ono Band. Yet millions of Beatles fans thought Yoko Ono was all wrong for John Lennon. Her exotic Japanese features, black clothes, and long messy hair that nearly covered her face made Yoko seem a little forbidding. When she and Lennon made music together, the result was shrill and coarse—quite different from the gentle ballads John wrote for the Beatles. Soon there were reports of friction between the Beatles and the possibility of a break up. Many knew just who to blame—Yoko Ono, the so-called Fifth Beatle.

Yet Yoko and John loved one another, and they were married in 1969. Yoko Ono had done many difficult things during her lifetime but, as she said years later, marrying one of the world's most famous men was the hardest. As an avant-garde artist, Ono often faced controversy but she at least expected to be taken seriously. Now, as John Lennon's wife, she saw herself turned into a cartoon villain. As her fame grew, she began to feel lost and alone. It reminded her of a difficult time in her own childhood.

Born into a wealthy family in Japan, Yoko Ono was surrounded by servants and tutors, but she almost never saw her own parents. She was a little girl who had everything and, at the same time, nothing. In her memory she can still see the long dining-room table in her family's Tokyo estate. There were chairs for every member of her large extended family, yet Yoko, called to her meals by a servant, ate alone. Her private tutor stood silently beside her.

Yoko Ono remembers, too, the parties her mother gave in those years before the hardships of World War II. All of Tokyo's high society came, glittering with priceless jewels and dressed like the Hollywood film stars of the day. She watched hidden from view as her parents and their friends sipped Champagne and smoked cigarettes from long holders.

The Ono family suffered during World War II, just as most Japanese people did. They were forced to flee the city and move to the countryside, where they often went without food. Shortly after the war Mr. Ono began a new job with the Bank of Tokyo and eventually was transferred to New York City. Yoko Ono, who was already an acclaimed musician and artist in Japan, decided to accompany her parents to New York. Ever since her arrival in the late 1940s, New York City and Yoko Ono have made deep impressions on one another.

John and Yoko liked to document their love story in a series of performance pieces. In order to promote world peace, they invited the world press to watch them for several days in their hotel room at the Amsterdam Hilton. They published intimate photographs of each other. Yet their marriage eventually ran into difficulties, and during the early 1970s they lived apart. In 1975, long after the Beatles had broken up, John and Yoko began living together again in New York City's Dakota apartment building. Their son, Sean, was born that year on John's own birthday, October 9.

On December 8, 1980, John and Yoko were returning home following a late session at a recording studio. They had been finishing work on a new album, *Double Fantasy*. Just in front of the Dakota a lone gunman approached the two and then, while Yoko watched helplessly, he shot and killed John.

Since that day the world has openly expressed both grief for John Lennon and sympathy for Yoko Ono. Just a few months after John's death, Yoko—who had never wanted to be known as just the wife of a pop singer—realized that only she could represent John's interests in the huge enterprise called The Beatles. She devoted herself to the job of handling requests for books, records, and films, always trying to make sure that John's image was handled fairly. As a single mother, she struggled to keep a wall of privacy around herself and Sean. In recent years one of Yoko Ono's greatest joys has been helping Sean and his band, Ima, in the recording studio. It reminded her, she told an interviewer, of when she and John worked together. She loved every second of it.

Seiji Ozawa

Conductor
1935–

As a boy growing up in Japan, Seiji Ozawa's first and only contact with European music was the sweet sound of his mother singing Christian hymns. So when he announced that he wanted to learn to play the piano, his family and teachers were stunned. Why the piano? Why not a traditional Japanese instrument? Despite their disapproval, his parents found a school that would teach him classical piano in the European style.

Born in Shenyang, China, in 1935, Seiji Ozawa was the third son in the family. In 1944, toward the end of World War II, he and his family moved back to Japan. Seiji and his three brothers studied music at an early age and were exposed to European as well as American musical traditions. Like many musicians, his talent was apparent very early. By the age of eighteen he was well prepared to enter Tokyo's prestigious Toho Gakuen School of Music.

After breaking a finger in a soccer game, Ozawa was forced to give up playing piano for several months and switched instead to composing and conducting. From this new experience he learned that he liked conducting music more than playing it and that he was good at it. When he won first prize in both conducting and composing, he decided to become an orchestra conductor.

After graduating from the Toho Gakuen School, Ozawa followed the advice of his favorite teacher, who thought that he should get his training conducting classical European music with the great orchestras of Europe. Although Seiji Ozawa spoke only Japanese, he decided to move to Paris to realize his ambitions. In 1959 he persuaded a Japanese motor scooter company to let him promote its scooter by riding one throughout Europe. Then he got passage on a freighter to Italy. Once there, he hopped on his scooter and headed for France. Within a year he had won first prize at the International Competition of Orchestra Conductors in Besançon.

This prize brought Seiji Ozawa to the attention of some of the best teachers in Europe. He studied one year in Paris and one year in Berlin. In 1960 he won a scholarship to play and study in the United States. It was at the Berkshire Music Center in Lenox, Massachusetts, that he was first noticed by the conductor of the New York Philharmonic Orchestra, Leonard Bernstein. Once Seiji Ozawa met the dynamic American maestro, his career began to move very fast. He was offered a job as assistant conductor for the New York Philharmonic and made his first professional concert appearance in North America in January 1962 with the San Fransisco Symphony.

A year later Ozawa returned to Japan as a guest conductor with Japan's best-known orchestra, the NHK Symphony. What should have been a triumphant moment for Ozawa, however, turned into an unhappy experience when musicians refused to play for him. Many were offended by his "showy" style and felt that he was not displaying traditional Japanese respect. A war of words followed that did not end until a special concert was scheduled by those wishing to mend the wounds. On that occasion Sieji Ozawa brilliantly conducted the Japanese Symphony Orchestra. He has been a popular guest conductor in Japan ever since.

After his Japanese tour Ozawa went back to the United States. He was named music director of the Chicago Symphony Orchestra's Ravinia Festival for five summers, from 1964 to 1968. During the winters he was music director for the Toronto Symphony Orchestra in Canada. He served as music director of the San Francisco Symphony from 1970 to 1976 and was later named the orchestra's music adviser. In 1973 Ozawa was also named music director of the Boston Symphony Orchestra.

As head of the Boston Symphony Orchestra, a position he held for nearly thirty years, Seiji Ozawa appeared regularly in the great music capitals of the world—Paris, Milan, Berlin, Salzburg. In Japan he is a role model for up-and-coming musicians; in America and Europe he is admired as one of the Western world's great classical conductors. Ozawa admits that, even today, nearly fifty years after first beginning his musical study in the West, he is still solidly Japanese in his outlook. Yet his love for the European musical tradition crosses racial and national barriers. Ozawa said, "Western music is like the sun. All over the world, the sunset is different, but the beauty is the same."

Seiji Ozawa left his position with the Boston Symphony Orchestra in 2002. He continues to travel the world as a guest conductor and as music director of the Vienna State Opera, but he still keeps his home near Boston. After so many years, he told a reporter, his house has too many memories to leave. He is also, by his own admission, a sports fanatic and returns to Massachusetts to keep track of his favorite teams, the Boston Red Sox, the Boston Celtics, and the New England Patriots.

Zubin Mehta

Conductor
1936–

The Mehta family knew their son Zubin was musically gifted, but they worried that a career in music would lead him nowhere. Medicine, his mother believed, was the field he should enter. When Zubin was assigned to dissect a lizard in a college biology class, he abruptly left the school. It was a gentle rebellion, the future maestro insists. He knew he was meant to be a musician and that it was silly to pretend anything else.

Musical talent was not just a fluke in the Mehta family. Zubin's father, Mehti Mehta, was a violinist and conductor as well as an active promoter of Western classical music in India. He had founded the Bombay String Quartet and the Bombay Symphony. As Zubin Mehta remembered, he was "brainwashed with classical music from the cradle." By the time he was sixteen he had already conducted the Bombay Symphony himself.

After two years of medical college, Zubin left for Vienna, where he enrolled in that city's most prestigious music school, the Academy of Music. At twenty-one he was awarded a diploma in conducting. A year later, in 1958, he entered the Liverpool International Conductor's Competition and won first prize. This award gave him a year's contract to conduct fourteen concerts of the Royal Liverpool Philharmonic. His reviews were always wildly enthusiastic.

By the early 1960s Zubin Mehta was flying around the world as guest conductor for the greatest orchestras. In 1961 the Los Angeles Philharmonic offered him the job of music director. He then became, at twenty-six, the youngest person ever to hold that job. A year later he was named conductor of the Montreal Symphony and became the first person ever to lead two major orchestras at the same time.

Mehta settled in Los Angeles and greatly enjoyed his life in the glittering film capital. Young, handsome, and much sought after by other celebrities, he became something of a matinee idol. Zubin Mehta's personality, described as "always in motion," suited Los Angeles as well.

Fate, however, was to take him from the West Coast to the East—from Los Angeles to New York City. In 1978 the New York Philharmonic asked Zubin Mehta to be their director, replacing the esteemed Pierre Boulez. Although Boulez was a hard act to follow, Mehta rose to the occasion. He remained the Philharmonic's musical director for thirteen years—the longest tenure of any director in the twentieth century. By 1990, however, administrative wrangling and bad press caused him to announce his resignation. He gave his farewell concert in May 1991.

That same year Zubin Mehta returned to his home in Los Angeles and resumed his active lifestyle. Today he continues to jet around the world, landing sometimes in Israel, where he holds a lifetime appointment as music director of the Israel Philharmonic, or in Montreal, Munich, or New York. Zubin Mehta simply travels, he says, "where there is a need to make music."

Allen Say

Artist, Illustrator, Photographer
1937–

In 1984, when a children's book editor telephoned Allen Say and asked him to illustrate a new book called *The Boy of the Three-Year Nap,* the answer was a resounding, "No!" Allen Say was tired of illustrating and wanted to do other things—maybe write a novel. But three years later, when the editor called again, the reluctant artist said yes.

Allen Say decided that if he was going to illustrate one more children's book, he would at least have fun with it. He locked himself in his studio, took out his old paint box, and began. As he worked, he began reliving many of his childhood memories in Japan and the experiences that led to his becoming an artist. He rediscovered the joy of using his old bamboo brush, a skill he had learned from Noro Shinpei, a great Japanese cartoonist. He discovered, too, that painting was his life's work and that, even at age fifty, he had much more to learn.

Say credits *The Boy of the Three-Year Nap* with helping him to grow as an artist. He modestly hopes that one day he might become very good at painting. If that happens, he says, "I would like to sign my work as my great hero, Hokusai, did . . . Old man crazy about drawing.' "[19]

Born in Yokohama, Japan, in 1937, Allen Say was painting at an early age. When he was twelve, he moved to nearby Tokyo to apprentice with Noro Shinpei. At age sixteen he moved to California, where he enrolled in the Los Angeles Center School. He continued his art studies at the University of California, Berkeley, and the San Francisco Art Institute, where he broadened his talents by becoming an accomplished photographer.

Books written and illustrated by Allen Say include *Under the Cherry Blossom Tree* (1974), *The Inn-Keeper's Apprentice* (1979), *The Bicycle Man* (1982), *The Tree of Cranes* (1991), and *Grandfather's Journey* (1993), a story of his own grandfather and the rich traditions of his Japanese ancestry. *Grandfather's Journey* was awarded the Caldecott Medal in 1994. In addition, Say has illustrated such books as *The Lucky Yak* by Eve Bunting (1980), as well as *The Boy of the Three-Year Nap* by Dianne Snyder, for which he was awarded the 1988 Boston Globe/Horn Book Award for best picture book. Allen Say's most recent book is *Home of the Brave* (2002), which is about life in a Japanese internment camp during World War II.

Bette Bao Lord

Writer
1938—

It is no wonder Bette Bao Lord likes to write about life's strange twists and turns—her own has been full of them. Born in Shanghai, China, just before the start of World War II, Bette Bao's father, Sandys, worked as an electrical engineer. After the war, in 1945, Sandys was sent by the Chinese Nationalist government to the United States so he could learn about the new technology that would help rebuild war-torn China. A year later he sent for his wife, Dora, and two daughters, Bette and Cathy. They traveled all the way to Brooklyn, New York, where Sandys Bao was working. A baby girl named Sansan was too young to travel and was left behind with relatives.

About her arrival in New York, Bette Bao later wrote: "I docked in Brooklyn on a sleepy Sunday and was enrolled at P.S. 8 in Brooklyn Heights on a sneezy Monday. Dopey and bashful was I because I didn't speak a word of English." And yet, despite a rocky start in her new country, when she returned to China in 1985, she was a well-known Chinese American author of books for both adults and children, all written in the language that had once seemed so impossible—English. She was also the wife of Winston Lord, a prominent American diplomat, who had just been named the U.S. ambassador to the People's Republic of China.

When Chinese Communists took over the government of China in 1949, Bette's parents realized they could not return to their homeland. They moved from Brooklyn to New Jersey, where Bette Bao attended high school. She later enrolled at Tufts University in Massachusetts, where she planned to study chemistry. She soon realized, however, that her talents lay elsewhere and changed her major to history and political science. In 1960 she received her master's degree from Tufts' Fletcher School of Law and Diplomacy. Two years later she married Winston Lord, a Tufts classmate who had entered the U.S. Foreign Service.

That same year, 1962, Bette Bao Lord was reunited with her sister, Sansan, whom she had not seen in sixteen years. As the sisters talked, Bette took pages of notes about Sansan's difficult life, which was so different from her own. At the suggestion of a publisher, Bette began writing about Sansan's years of manual labor and near starvation and about the painful reunion with her parents and sister. *Eighth Moon,* published in 1964, was a best-seller and was translated into fifteen languages.

In the years following the publication of *Eighth Moon,* Bette Lord raised a family and participated as an unofficial member of her husband's diplomatic team. Following a trip to China with Winston Lord in 1973, Bette Lord began her next book, a novel called *Spring Moon.* Writing this saga of a Chinese family was, she remembered, one of the most difficult things she had ever done. Yet despite six years of what she called the "agony of the blank page," the book was finally published in 1981 and nominated the next year for the prestigious American Book Award.

Her next book—her first for young readers—was a lighthearted story of a young Chinese girl growing up in Brooklyn in the 1940s. *In the Year of the Boar and Jackie Robinson* introduces us to Shirley Temple Wong, who, very much like Bette Bao herself, sails across the sea with her mother to join her father in New York. It describes the trials of a young Chinese girl struggling to understand life in America. Once again, her book was a great success.

In 1985 Winston Lord was named the U.S. Ambassador to China and the family returned to Bette Bao's homeland. Although it was Winston who had taken the oath of office, Bette became his unofficial adviser and interpreter. Just before leaving China in 1989, she witnessed firsthand the powerful student democracy movement and its tragic ending when many young people were killed on Beijing's Tiananmen Square. Shaken by all she had seen and heard during her four years in her native country, she wrote *Legacies: A Chinese Mosaic*, about the lives of relatives, old friends, and new friends. In 1996 she published her second novel, *The Middle Heart*.

Today the Lords live in New York City, where they write and lecture. Bette Lord works with the Freedom Forum, which fosters the exchange of ideas, research, and cultures throughout the world.

Maxine Hong Kingston

Writer
1940–

"I come from the tradition of storytellers," Maxine Hong Kingston once wrote, "and that tradition is thousands of years old; but I'm different from the others in that I write, whereas the rest of them used memory and the moods of the audience . . ."[20] Maxine Hong's "tradition" came from her mother, Yin Lan Hong—known in English as Brave Orchid—who told the legends, myths, and history of the people of Kwangzou, Canton, while she cleaned and pressed clothes in their Stockton, California, laundry. Brave Orchid's talk-stories became the source of Maxine Hong Kingston's later work.

Maxine Hong's parents never thought they would raise their children in a laundry. Her father, born near the Chinese city of Canton, was a scholar and poet. He was a teacher of Chinese literature when, in 1924, he decided to leave for the United States. He said good-bye to his wife, who was then studying medicine, and moved to New York City. After months of looking for work as a teacher, he finally took his first job in a Chinese laundry.

Soon after Yin Lan Hong joined her husband in America, the couple decided to make a fresh start in Stockton. After a few years of working at odd jobs, they were able to buy their own business, the New Port Laundry. New Port was the center of family life for Maxine Hong and her five younger brothers and sisters, and they seldom left it. They were completely comfortable there, working and playing alongside their parents and the Chinese customers. School, on the other hand, was a source of daily pain.

It spite of being born in California, when Maxine entered kindergarten in Stockton she knew so little about the language and culture of the United States that she could barely understand the teacher's hand gestures. She remembers that for several years in grade school she did not say a word: "During the first silent year I spoke to no one at school, did not ask before going to the lavatory, and flunked kindergarten. . . . I enjoyed the silence."[21]

A sensitive, generous sixth-grade teacher brought Maxine Hong out of her silent world and into the academic one, in which she eventually excelled. After graduating from the University of California at Berkeley and teaching for several years in Hawaii, Maxine Hong Kingston (she had married a college boyfriend, Earll Kingston) began her career as a professional writer. Brave Orchid's talk-stories had been turning over and over in her mind, and she set them down in her first book, *The Woman Warrior: Memoirs of a Girlhood Among Ghosts* (1976).

The "ghosts" in her book's title are the many mysterious, frightening elements of her girlhood: the incomprehensible white people of Stockton;

the spirits of her Chinese ancestors; and the powerful women of Brave Orchid's talk-stories, who accepted lives of slavery to their husbands, fathers, and grown sons. "What is it that's a story," Hong tries to find out, "And what is it that's life?"

In her next book, *China Men,* she confronts the history of Chinese men in the United States. "Claiming America" is how she describes her mission in this book. Claiming it, that is, for those who worked so hard clearing sugarcane fields in Hawaii or hacking away at the granite faces of the Sierra Nevada to lay the track for the transcontinental railroad. Again she tries to right the wrongs of the past, this time those of American society, which fought so long to exclude the Chinese.

Her third book and first novel, *Tripmaster Monkey: His Fake Book,* was published in 1989. Maxine has also written poems, stories, and essays. After having lived nearly twenty years in Hawaii, Maxine Hong Kingston and her husband moved to Oakland, California, in 1989. Today she continues to write, teach, and lecture around the world.

Bruce Lee

Martial Artist, Actor
1940–1973

In movie after movie Bruce Lee kicked and chopped his way through the menacing underworlds of Asia and America. A man of remarkable discipline and martial arts skill, he became a true hero to millions of moviegoers of all ages around the world.

Born in San Francisco, Bruce Lee was the son of Lee Hoi Chuen, a star of the Chinese opera. Bruce was raised in Hong Kong, where he became a well-known child actor. At thirteen he began studying kung fu, a Chinese martial art used for self-defense. At eighteen he returned to the United States to study philosophy at the University of Washington in Seattle. While in college, he opened his own kung fu academy.

In 1964 Bruce Lee traveled to Long Beach, California, to give a demonstration at the International Karate Championship. There he was noticed by the producer of the television series *Batman*. Impressed with Lee's skills, the producer offered him the role of Kato in the show. Bruce Lee later also appeared in the television series *The Green Hornet*, which ran during the late 1960s. Lee soon became disillusioned with Hollywood and the stereotypical roles he was usually offered. When he was overlooked for the lead role in the TV series *Kung Fu*—a white actor was chosen instead—Bruce Lee returned to Hong Kong.

During the 1960s thousands of kung fu movies were made in Hong Kong. Most were geared to the so-called Mandarin circuit, which included Hong Kong, Singapore, Indonesia, and Taiwan. The typical kung fu film was short on dialogue and character development but full of action. Bruce Lee's films, however, while loaded with scenes of the fast-kicking, fast-chopping star taking on creepy underworld figures, also allowed him to act. After appearing in just a few Hong Kong-made films, Bruce Lee became an international box-office sensation.

Audiences were dazzled by Bruce Lee's kung fu skills. This, they knew, was not the usual actor practicing the martial arts but a true artist. Bruce Lee called his highly personal, and much copied, karate style *jeet kune do*, or "intercepting fist way."

Bruce Lee believed karate was part of an inner journey. "It's an art," he once said, "and in learning it you learn about yourself. The punch or kick is not just to knock the other guy over, but to kick at your own ego, your fears. With the ego out of the way," he reminded young students, "you can express yourself clearly."

Bruce Lee was already a huge star in Asia when his movies became popular in the United States. *Fists of Fury* and *The Iron Hand* are just two that broke box-office records. *Enter the Dragon*, the first kung fu movie made in Hong Kong specifically for American audiences, promised to make Bruce Lee a superstar here, too.

On July 21, 1973, however, just before the release of *Enter the Dragon,* Bruce Lee died in Hong Kong of a brain aneurysm. He left his wife, Linda, a white American, and two children, Brandon and Shannon. At his funeral in Hong Kong thousands of screaming fans tried to break through police barricades to get closer to their fallen hero. Lee's burial was in Seattle, Washington, where today many pay homage to the immortal master.

Dith Pran

Journalist
1942–

The story is by now familiar even though its horror is undiminished. In April 1975 the government of Cambodia fell and the U.S.-backed army fled the country. The Communist-led forces of the Khmer Rouge, led by Pol Pot, took over this Southeast Asian nation. As the capital city of Phnom Penh lay under seige, *New York Times* correspondent Sydney Schanberg and his assistant, Dith Pran, who were covering the story, took refuge in the French embassy. A few days later Schanberg was allowed to leave Cambodia; Dith Pran, unable to secure the necessary papers, walked out of the embassy and into the Cambodian countryside.

Dith Pran was born in 1942 in the Siem Reap township near the ruins of the great temple complex of Angkor Wat in Cambodia. He came from a very close-knit family.

From an early age, Pran had a gift for languages. He learned French in high school and taught himself English at home. After graduating from high school, he became a translator for a U.S. military assistance group in Cambodia. Dith Pran had to find a new job in 1965, however, when the Cambodian government asked all U.S. advisers to leave the country. By then, war was raging in neighboring Vietnam, and Cambodian premier Norodom Sihanouk feared that Americans who were working inside Cambodia might overthrow the government.

For a while Pran became an interpreter for a British film crew that was working on a film in the area. Later he became a trilingual receptionist at one of the best-known tourist hotels. But by 1970 Cambodia, too, was at war, and the country's valuable tourist trade had completely stopped. Once again Pran was out of work.

There were, however, many foreign journalists who had flocked to Phnom Penh to cover the expanding war. Pran and his wife, Ser Moeun, and their children moved to the capital so Pran could work as a guide and a translator. It was there that Pran met *New York Times* reporter Sydney Schanberg.

Dith Pran was thirty in 1972 when he first started to work with Sydney Schanberg. By then he already had served as a guide and an interpreter to several *New York Times* reporters. Everyone recommended him. His English and French were both excellent, and his understanding of Cambodian culture was invaluable. Pran knew who to see, who to talk to, and how to gain entry into Cambodia's closed circles.

Sydney Schanberg was quickly impressed with Pran's efficiency and thoroughness. The two became trusted friends. In 1973 Schanberg asked the *New York Times* to make Dith Pran a full-time stringer, or news assistant. From then on Pran worked only for Schanberg, much to the dismay of other reporters who wanted to benefit from his expertise.

Early in 1973 it had become clear that Americans were preparing to withdraw completely from both Cambodia and Vietnam. They mistakenly believed that a peace settlement, signed in Paris that January, would end the long conflict. But the war dragged on for two more years, leading to the tragic events that began with the closing of the U.S. embassy in Phnom Penh on April 14, 1975. Pran and Schanberg watched as the last American Marine helicopter evacuated all remaining personnel from the doomed capital.

Two days earlier, Pran and Schanberg had said good-bye to Pran's wife and four children, who had flown to San Francisco to wait for Pran's arrival. Pran and Schanberg were to stay only a few additional days to cover the end of the war. As the situation in Phnom Penh grew increasingly confused, however, and a Communist takeover seemed imminent, Schanberg and Pran—ever the good journalists—drove around the city trying to take its pulse. At one point they were pulled over by Khmer Rouge soldiers who seemed quite prepared to kill them. Pran began talking, however, and talked nonstop until the soldiers decided to let the car drive on. Sydney Schanberg credited Pran's persuasive speech with saving their lives.

The two drove quickly to the safety of the French embassy, which they entered by scaling its tall fence. French officials tried to help Pran, but when they realized the Khmer would kill everyone in the embassy if they believed any Cambodian citizens were inside, they insisted he go. As Dith Pran left the embassy compound, Sydney Schanberg pounded his fists on the cold stone wall, distraught that he was not able to save his friend.

A few days later Schanberg returned to the United States, going first to San Francisco to break the news to Pran's wife. Dith Pran's journey of survival, however, had just begun. He first assumed the role of a lowly taxi driver, not letting on that he was an educated man, a fact that could have cost him his life. Eventually he was taken prisoner and spent most of the next four years in one of Pol Pot's concentration camps, enduring unspeakable horrors.

In late 1978, the Vietnamese Communists invaded Cambodia and forced the blood-thirsty Pol Pot out of office. With the Khmer Rouge gone, starving, diseased Cambodians began to emerge from the concentration camps. On October 3, 1979, Pran crossed the border into Thailand and made his way to the United States.

On January 20, 1980, Dith Pran's story appeared in the *New York Times* magazine. The article, called "The Death and Life of Dith Pran," described the fall of Cambodia and Sydney Schanberg's search for his friend. It opened the eyes of millions of people to Cambodia's tragedy. It also made Dith Pran a celebrity. He was asked to give lectures, write books, and appear on television. In 1983 he and Sydney Schanberg agreed to allow their story to be made into a movie called *The Killing Fields*. The movie premiered in 1984. The following year it won an Academy Award for Best Picture. Dr. Haing Ngor, who portrayed Dith Pran in the film, won an Oscar for Best Supporting Actor.

Dith Pran is now a citizen of the United States and, since 1980, has been a staff news photographer for the *New York Times*. In 1989 he returned to Cambodia, and his journey was described in an article, "Return to the Killing Fields," which appeared in the *New York Times* magazine. During his visit Pran released 200 pigeons into the air above Phnom Penh and watched as they circled the city before flying away. According to Cambodian legend, if you free a captive animal, it will carry a message of peace to the rest of the world. As founder of the Dith Pran Holocaust Awareness Project and as Goodwill Ambassador for the UN High Commission for Refugees, Pran speaks for those who did not survive and for those who still suffer. "I don't consider myself a politician or a hero," he says simply. "I am a messenger."

Internment Camp Inmates

1942–1945

On February 19, 1942, just two months after the United States went to war with the Japanese following their bombing of Pearl Harbor in Hawaii, President Franklin Delano Roosevelt signed Executive Order 9066. It authorized military authorities to remove all people of Japanese ancestry living on the West Coast and incarcerate them in camps set up in remote areas of the country for the duration of the war. The order, which directly affected about 120,000 Japanese Americans, 80,000 of whom were American citizens, was later judged racially motivated and a violation of their constitutional rights. This judgment, however, came too late to correct the wrongs that have had lasting consequences even to the present day.

Notices ordering the removal of Japanese Americans were posted on walls and buildings, printed in newspapers, and announced on the radio. The head of each family was ordered to report to a Civil Control Center to pick

A line of Japanese American internees line up for a meal at the internment camp in Puyallup, Washington.

up numbered tags that were to be worn by each member of the family and attached to the two suitcases and one duffle bag that each person was allowed to take to the camp. All other belongings had to be sold, stored, or thrown away. Many families had to sell their houses and businesses. Some were cheated by greedy speculators. Each had a week to get ready but had no idea how long they would be imprisoned during the war.

Japanese reactions to removal varied widely. While most felt they had no real alternative but to accept the executive order, others resisted imprisonment, and a few actually challenged its constitutionality in court.

Fearing that total opposition to removal might lead to violence and bloodshed, the Japanese American Citizens League (JACL) advised Japanese Americans to cooperate, "under protest," with the order. Most did. In fact, most people believed that cooperating with the government edict was the best way to help the country at the time.

As dazed Japanese Americans prepared, the U.S. government began building the detention camps on unused federal lands in remote desert or swamp areas. Eventually, there were ten detention camps: Topaz in Utah, Poston and Gila in Arizona, Manzanar and Tule Lake in California, Minidoka in Idaho, Granada in Colorado, Rohwer and Jerome in Arkansas, and Heart Mountain in Wyoming. Each camp housed between 5,000 and 20,000 Issei (Japanese immigrants who were restricted by U.S. law from becoming U.S. citizens and their American-born children).

Before moving to the camps, the angry, frightened Japanese Americans were taken to makeshift relocation centers near large cities. These quarters were former fairgrounds, racetracks, or livestock halls, where animal stalls were quickly cleaned and painted for human occupancy.

By the summer of 1942, permanent camps were completed and Japanese Americans were transported there by train. Upon arriving at the camps, they were shocked to find row upon row of black tar-paper barracks the size of chicken houses surrounded by endless barbed-wire fences patrolled by armed soldiers. In Western camps, such as those in Utah, California, and Arizona, people would have to suffer through hot dusty summers and below-zero winters. In southern camps, they would have to contend with damp, swampy lowlands and hot, humid temperatures.

As the initial shock of the primitive camps began to wear off and imprisonment became a way of life, people began organizing schools, health clinics, recreational facilities, and governing boards. Work projects were started, and a certain camp routine was established.

Top: Evacuees arrive in the first Japanese evacuation colony in California. Bottom: Cars left behind by Japanese Americans upon arrival at the colony.

Although camps took on the activities of small, self-sufficient towns, there was nothing normal about camp life. The conditions were terrible: five to eight people lived in bare, 20-by 25-foot (6-by 8-m) rooms with no privacy. Three hundred inmates shared a mess hall, laundry, showers, latrine, and recreation hall. Until inmates began taking responsibility for life in the camps, food was bad and boredom a constant problem.

In the midst of all the tension and frustration, camps had to run smoothly and basic services had to be provided. Some camps grew their own food. In larger camps, factories were set up. Because families were given only $7.50 a month as an allowance, people needed to work just to earn enough money for necessities.

The most valued jobs were those connected to release programs, which contracted Nisei (second generation) men out to farmers who needed laborers to harvest crops. These jobs allowed men the freedom to be outside the camps. Young people also were allowed temporary release from camps to attend college.

By February 1943 some young Nisei men were volunteering from the camps to fight in World War II in an elite, all-Japanese American regiment called the 442nd Regimental Combat Team. The team, which had been established as an experimental regiment composed of second-generation Japanese Americans and white officers, would eventually become one of the most highly decorated units of the war. Nisei distinguished themselves as scouts and as interpreters in the Pacific War and as an elite fighting machine on both the Pacific and European fronts. Often volunteering against the wishes of their parents and under criticism of many camp elders, Nisei believed that by serving in the war, they would win freedom for their families and eliminate prejudice against Japanese Americans.

Because of the valiant fighting of Nisei soldiers and gradual changes in the attitudes of American people, Japanese Americans slowly began regaining some of what racial discrimination and greed had unjustly taken from them. In December 1944 pending court cases were decided in favor of releasing Japanese American evacuees. Based on those decisions, and on the fact that the U.S. military no longer considered mass exclusion of West Coast Japanese necessary, it was announced that all the camps would be closed by the end of 1945.

By then, more than 30,000 people had already left the camps. By September 1945 about 15,000 people a month were leaving. Although most people were happy to finally regain their freedom, many protested the sudden closings of the camps. Those who had had to sell their farms and homes when the government imprisoned them now had nowhere to go. Many feared anti-Japanese treatment when they returned to their communities. Having already suffered mentally and financially, Japanese Americans rightly believed they should be given some type of government assistance. Their petitions were ignored, however, and they had to relocate on their own, with minimal assistance from the government.

Their struggle for compensation for wrongful imprisonment and loss of material gain continued until well into the 1980s. In the summer and fall of 1981, the Commission on Wartime Relocation and Internment of Civilians (CWRIC) held hearings on the imprisonment of Japanese Americans during World War II and concluded the following:

> The promulgation of Executive Order 9066 was not justified by military necessity, and the decisions which followed from it—detention, ending detention and ending exclusion—were not driven by analysis of military conditions. The broad historical causes which shaped these decisions were race, prejudice, war hysteria and a failure of political leadership.[22]

In August 1988 President Ronald Reagan signed a bill that offered an official apology to American citizens of Japanese ancestry and gave a payment of $20,000 to each survivor of the detention camps. He said that the imprisonment of Japanese Americans had been "a grave wrong" and the time had come to finish "a sad chapter in American history." It is indeed, a sad chapter, for such grave wrongs can never be made right.

Gordon Hirabayashi, Fred Korematsu, and Minoru Yasui

Internment Resistance Fighters

On April 30, 1942, General John L. De Witt issued the order that all persons of Japanese ancestry (American citizens as well as resident aliens of Japanese ancestry) were under immediate curfew and should await orders for removal to detention camps. Most obeyed without hesitation. Believing that cooperating with the government edict was the best way to help the country at the time, the Japanese American Citizens League (JACL) advised Japanese Americans to comply.

Three men in three different states, however, refused to obey the order and were sent to prison: Gordon Hirabayashi of Washington, Fred Korematsu of California, and Minoru Yasui of Oregon. Forty years later their convictions were overturned. Investigations in the 1980s by the Congressional Commission on Wartime Relocation and Internment of Civilians led to the

"Keep-Away sign at Topaz" (1943), watercolor by Chiura Obata. Such signs told camp inmates they would be shot on sight if they crossed the barbed–wire fence.

conclusion that the U.S. government not only had omitted giving pertinent information to the Supreme Court concerning these cases but had also misled the Supreme Court on matters of the "military necessity issue."

Gordon Hirabayashi, a native of Seattle, was a student at the University of Washington in 1942. During the first week or so of the 8:00 P.M. to 6:00 A.M. curfew, he dutifully rushed back from the library or work to his dorm. After a few days, however, he began to feel there was no reason he should have to be inside at 8:00 when none of his dorm mates were similarly affected. Believing that the principles of the Bill of Rights supported his decision to ignore orders that singled him out just because of his ethnic background, Hirabayashi began ignoring the curfew. He was prepared to go to prison rather than obey the orders.

Meanwhile in Portland, Oregon, a young lawyer named Minoru Yasui was making a similar decision. Guided by his own legal training, he reasoned that the curfew and internment orders were simply against the law. After talking with other attorneys and the Japanese American Citizens League, he decided to resist the order. On March 28 Yasui had a friend call the police and tell them he was not obeying the curfew. The police tried to ignore Yasui, who eventually walked into a Portland police station and forced the arrest. He intended to use his entire life savings of $5,000 to see his case through court.

Fred Korematsu's reasons for disobeying the army's orders were different still. He had no particular moral or legal qualms. He simply did not want to leave his Oakland, California, home for "personal" reasons. He, too, was arrested, tried, convicted, and eventually sent to prison.

In May of 1943 Gordon Hirabayashi's appeal was heard by the U.S. Supreme Court. In June the eight justices handed down their decision, agreeing unanimously with the ruling of the Washington State court. They felt that "national safety" concerns were, at the time, more pressing than

Gordon Hirabayashi testifying before the Commission on Wartime Relocation and Internment of Civilians.

issues of racial discrimination. The courts reached the same conclusions in the cases of Korematsu and Yasui.

In 1981, however, all three men were told by a lawyer at the University of California, San Diego, that evidence had been uncovered suggesting that in 1942 the War Department had deliberately changed the wording of its original evacuation order. The difference seemed minor, but to legal scholars it was significant enough to make the cases worth retrying.

Two years later courts in California and Oregon dismissed both the Korematsu and Yasui cases after "vacating" (to make legally void) the original convictions. A judge in Seattle, however, decided not to dismiss the case against Gordon Hirabayashi. Instead, he handed down an important ruling, saying that because the War Department changed the wording of General

De Witt's original order, the court cases had never been pleaded correctly. The judge left open the possibility that the evacuation order might have been found illegal and stopped by the Supreme Court.

The legal battles of Fred Korematsu, Gordon Hirabayashi, and Minoru Yasui helped to uncover the truth about a racially motivated period in U.S. history and to correct the political and legal mistakes that were perpetuating discrimination. Their efforts contributed to the passage of legislation that eventually compensated, though never adequately, for Japanese American losses. In 1948 Congress passed the Japanese American Evacuation Claims Act that appropriated funds to reimburse Japanese Americans for their losses. President Gerald Ford issued Presidential Proclamation 4417 in 1976, both rescinding and apologizing for Executive Order 9066. Finally Congress passed the Civil Liberties Act of 1988, authorizing compensation to living survivors of the camps.

Ellison S. Onizuka

Astronaut, Aerospace Engineer
1946–1986

On his first flight into space, Lt. Colonel Ellison S. Onizuka took along a few mementos. The Kona coffee and macadamia nuts were from the Hawaiian village where he was born and raised. The Buddhist medallion was from his father, who had instilled in him the values of patience, hard work, and dedication to duty. Ellison also took along patches from the Japanese American 442nd combat regiment, whose patriotism and courage during World War II were legendary. These same qualities had brought Onizuka to this point—to the lift-off of the space shuttle *Discovery* and to the fulfillment of all his dreams.

Ellison Onizuka was born on June 24, 1946, in Kealakekua, Hawaii. The grandson of Hawaiian plantation workers, Onizuka showed an early interest in flying and engineering. In 1964 he won a scholarship to the University of Colorado, where he majored in aerospace engineering and participated in the air force ROTC program.

In 1969, just before earning a master of science degree from Colorado, he married fellow Hawaiian Lorna Yoshida. As third-generation Japanese Americans, they were the first in their families to choose their own marriage partners, rather than have their parents decide. Onizuka became active in the air force, and just before the couple moved to the McClellan Air Force Base in Sacramento, California, their first daughter, Janelle, was born. A second girl, Darien, was born a few years later. At McClellan, Ellison Onizuka designed flight test programs and aircraft safety systems.

A short time later Ellison Onizuka was accepted into the competitive Air Force Test Pilot School at Edwards Air Force Base in California's Mojave Desert. At Edwards he tested aircraft and taught engineering to other pilots. His skills were noticed by air force and NASA officials, and he was invited to apply to the astronaut program. In the early 1970s NASA's focus had moved away from the *Apollo* moon missions to the *Skylab* space shuttles, for which many new specialists were needed.

Of the 8,100 candidates who applied for NASA's space-shuttle program, Ellison Onizuka was among the first 220 who were interviewed. His all-around qualifications led to his becoming one of the thirty-five men and women chosen for *Skylab*.

The Onizuka family moved to Houston, Texas, in 1978, where Onizuka could begin training at the Johnson Space Center. His schedule included classes in computers, astronomy, oceanography, and mathematics. He trained in a weightless atmosphere and practiced simulated lift-offs and landing procedures. Since Onizuka was a mission specialist, he also received training from the Department of Defense on various confidential technical assignments.

In 1982 Onizuka was one of five astronauts chosen for the flight of the *Discovery*, which was launched on January 24, 1985. The mission lasted only three days. The rounds of parades and public appearances, however, celebrating the first Asian American in space, lasted for months. After the *Discovery* flight, Ellison returned to Hawaii to visit both family and friends and to speak to schoolchildren throughout the islands.

By mid-1985 Lt. Colonel Onizuka was back in Houston training for his next mission, the flight of the *Challenger*. Unlike the *Discovery*, the *Challenger* assignment was not top secret. It was to carry seven men and women of various backgrounds, including a schoolteacher from New Hampshire named Christa McAuliffe. Her highly publicized participation meant that many Americans—especially schoolchildren—would be watching the televised lift-off from Florida's Kennedy Space Center the morning of January 28, 1986.

The fate of the *Challenger* is now a tragic part of American history. Seventy-three seconds after lift-off, a malfunction in the rocket booster caused it to blow up and disappear into the Atlantic Ocean just off the Florida coast. None of the *Challenger* crew survived.

Although Ellison Onizuka's life was cut short, he left behind an impressive legacy for those who strive to attain the impossible and create a better world. His dedication and personal goals are best remembered in a message he delivered to a group of high school graduates in Hawaii:

> Every generation has the obligation to free men's minds for a look at new worlds . . . to look out from a higher plateau than the last generation. . . . Make your life count—and the world will be a better place because you tried.[23]

Connie Chung

News Anchor, Reporter
1946–

When CBS-TV hired Connie Chung to be an on-air reporter in 1972, it seemed as though the network was just filling an ethnic quota. The Federal Communications Commission (FCC), which oversees radio and TV broadcasts, had been pressuring the major networks to hire more women and minorities. Connie often joked that by hiring her, CBS got a two-for-one deal. They also got, as television viewers soon discovered, an insightful, determined reporter.

Constance Yu-hwa Chung was the last of Margaret Wa and William Ling Chung's ten children and the only one born in the United States. The Chungs had fled Shanghai, China, in 1944, in the midst of a Japanese bombing raid. World War II had already taken its toll on the family; five children had died since the conflict had begun in 1941.

To prevent further harm to his family and to secure their future, Connie Chung's father moved his family to America. Trained as a diplomat, William Ling Chung became an official at the Chinese embassy in Washington, D.C. When the Communists took over mainland China, he began working for the embassy of the Nationalist Chinese of Taiwan.

Connie Chung grew up in Washington's Maryland suburbs. Despite coming from a traditional Chinese household, she spent her high school years learning to be a typical American girl. She acted in school plays and took part in student government. She also developed a keen interest in both American politics and world affairs.

In 1965, after graduating from the University of Maryland with a degree in journalism, Ms. Chung became a news department secretary at WITG, a Washington, D.C., television station. She advanced quickly, becoming a news writer, then an editor, and finally an on-air reporter. CBS's Washington bureau noticed this bright young journalist and hired her as one of their first female reporters.

Connie Chung quickly distinguished herself as a tireless worker whom coworkers remembered as being willing to do anything for a story no matter how difficult or frightening. In 1976 the local CBS affiliate in Los Angeles hired Chung to be their news anchor. She appeared on the air three times a day and quickly became popular with viewers. She won numerous awards for broadcasting and became the highest paid local news anchor in the country.

By 1983, however, with a presidential election looming the next year, Connie was eager to get back into the arena of national politics. She accepted a job offer from NBC to anchor a morning news show, *NBC at Sunrise,* and the Saturday edition of *NBC Nightly News.* She left CBS and Los Angeles and moved across the country to New York City.

At NBC Connie was involved with the network's attempt to start a newsmagazine to rival CBS's highly successful *Sixty Minutes.* In 1985 she became the chief correspondent for a show called *American Almanac* and a later one called simply *1986*. Neither of these clicked with viewers, although three hour-long news specials produced by Connie were well received.

In March 1989 Connie announced she would return to CBS, where she had been offered an annual salary of $1.5 million to host her own show, *Saturday Night with Connie Chung*, and to be a substitute for lead anchor, Dan Rather. She eventually became coanchor of the *CBS Evening News* before being hired away by ABC, who asked her to host their popular newsmagazine *20/20*. At the beginning of 2002 Connie Chung moved to CNN, the Cable News Network.

Throughout her long career Chung has won many prestigious awards, including three Emmys. She currently lives in New York City with her husband, television host Maury Povich, and their son, Matthew.

Lawrence Yep

Writer
1948–

Born on the fringes of San Francisco's Chinatown and a black ghetto, Lawrence Yep knew nothing about white America until he entered high school. And then, surrounded by three very different cultures, he felt cast off by all of them. This sense of alienation explains his early interest in writing science fiction. In science fiction, after all, the creator can start fresh and make up an entirely new culture—something Lawrence Yep wanted to do all along.

After graduating from the University of California at Santa Cruz in 1970, Yep went on to earn a Ph.D. in English from the State University of New York at Buffalo. Soon after finishing college, he published his first book, *Sweetwater,* which tells the story of an early colonist from Earth who visits the star Harmony.

His best-known work, *Dragonwings,* named a Newbery Honor Book in 1975, is a combination of historical fiction and fantasy. It is set in early twentieth-century San Francisco and tells the story of a Chinese man named Windrider who fulfills a life's dream when in 1909 he builds and flies an airplane. Other children's books by Lawrence Yep include *Dragon's Gate,* a 1993 Newbery Honor Book; *Child of the Owl; Sea Glass;* and *Dragon of the Lost Sea.*

One of Yep's recent books, *The Star Fisher,* is based on his family's history. The main character, fifteen-year-old Joan Lee, is much like Yep's own mother. In the 1920s Lawrence Yep's grandparents, mother, aunts, and uncles left their home and laundry business in Ohio and moved to the small, remote city of Clarksburg, West Virginia, to start a new life. There they experienced discrimination from the townspeople and struggled to survive within two very distinct cultures, Chinese and American. Today Lawrence Yep lives in San Francisco with his wife, Joanne Ryder, a children's book author. He teaches writing at the University of California, Berkeley. Through his writing and storytelling, he continues to focus on Asian America and on what separates one culture, whether real or imaginary, from another.

June Kuramoto

Musician

1948–

June Okida Kuramoto first heard the magical sounds of the koto (a Japanese stringed instrument) when her mother took her to a concert performed by Madame Kazue Kudo in Los Angeles. After that memorable experience, June Okida begged her mother to let her learn how to play the koto from Madame Kudo. Her mother finally agreed, and the relationship between June Okida and Madame Kudo grew into a rich musical partnership.

June Okida was born in Saitama-ken, near Tokyo, Japan, and moved with her family to Los Angeles five years later. From the age of six, Okida took koto lessons once a week and practiced for at least an hour every day after school. Schoolmates made fun of her interest in the heavy, 6-foot-long instrument, which made what they called "grandma music." But June Okida was able to ignore their taunts. She studied traditional koto music with Madame Kudo and then went on to get her master's degree from the Michio Miyagi Koto School of Tokyo.

Between high school and college, June Okida began to develop a new musical style. As if in answer to the jeers of her classmates, Okida looked for ways to bring the rich sounds of the koto together with the unique strains of American rock and jazz. In her early twenties she began working with a jazz flutist named Dan Kuramoto, whom she married in 1971. Together they brought a new dimension to Dan's band, called Hiroshima. Besides the flute and koto, they eventually added keyboards, woodwinds, drums, bass, and guitar to create a musical style that was distinctly Asian American. Later they included both percussion and the Japanese taiko drums.

During the 1970s and the 1980s Hiroshima recorded six albums and toured often, playing in well-known big-city nightclubs. They received a Grammy nomination in 1981 and their album *Go* was named Best Jazz Album at the Soul Train Music Awards in 1988. It also was on the top of Billboard's Contemporary Jazz Album charts for eight weeks that same year.

Today, when not working with Hiroshima, Ms. Kuramoto tours and records with other well-known musical artists. Her koto music adds a special sound to the music of many contemporary pop and jazz artists. She has performed with Manhattan Transfer, Stanley Clarke, Martika, Foreigner, and Teddy Pendergrass. June Kuramoto, true to her early training, has also performed with classical musicians, from India's Ravi Shankar to Japan's greatest masters.

In 1989 she and other members of Hiroshima appeared in a play called *Sansei* (third-generation Japanese Americans). Based on their own experiences growing up in Los Angeles, the play was a kind of portrait of Japanese

American life in music and drama. June and Dan Kuramoto have also written scores for television and film, including *The Thin Red Line* and *Black Rain*. Recent CDs include *The Best of Hiroshima* (1994) and *Beyond Black and White* (1999), which they recorded for the Windham Hill Jazz label.

"I see myself as a human being first, then a musician," June Kuramoto once told an interviewer. All her life, her goal has been to move away from the stereotyped view of Asian Americans and focus instead on their rich cultural heritage. Through her instrumental music and songs, June Kuramoto is achieving this goal. Although she has been criticized by some in the Asian community for combining classical koto music and Western instruments, many strongly support her work and identify with her generous approach to musical styles.

Wayne Wang

Film Director
1949–

Wayne Wang was born in Hong Kong six days after his parents escaped from Communist China. It was a rocky start by any standards. But Wang's father, who had once been a prosperous merchant in his native Tsingtao, had one considerable advantage. He had learned English while selling merchandise to American sailors at a naval base near Tsingtao. Later it would be key to the success of his fledgling import-export business.

Although the Wangs did prosper in Hong Kong, they were never happy there. Once they resigned themselves to the fact that they might never return to their homeland, they began to look hopefully toward America.

In 1968 Wayne Wang moved to America to attend college and to, as he laughingly described it, "become American." While in graduate school at the California College of Arts and Crafts, he studied film production. But he saw little chance of breaking into the filmmaking business in the highly competitive Los Angeles area, so he returned to Hong Kong. There he became the director of a popular television series.

Still eager to do serious filmmaking, he and his wife, Cora Miao, returned to the United States where they immediately began work on a film called *Chan Is Missing*. Wang hoped the film would speak to young Asian Americans who might be just as mixed up as he was about whether to be more "Asian" or more "American." The low-budget film, which cost just $22,000 to make, was released in 1983. It won the attention of many critics who acknowledged its gentle humor.

His next film, *Dim Sum*, cost four times as much as his first film. It proved much more difficult to make because he had to decide whether he wanted to create a slick, commercially successful movie or a gentle story about characters he knew and loved. Halfway through production of the film, he shifted gears and focused on the latter—the relationship between a daughter and her widowed mother.

Dim Sum was completed in May 1985 and shown that same year at the Cannes Film Festival. It confirmed what critics and moviegoers already knew about Wayne Wang—that he is a graceful, sensitive artist who is able to portray Chinese American life in a humorous and yet tender way. One critic said that in Wang's movies there is enough room for both Confucius and American soap operas.

Since the success of *Dim Sum*, Wayne Wang's fame has grown. He completed *Eat a Bowl of Tea* (1989) and then *The Joy Luck Club* (1993), based on the novel by Amy Tan. Other films include *Smoke* and *Blue in the Face* (1995); *Chinese Box* (1997), starring Jeremy Irons and filmed in Hong Kong; and *Anywhere but Here* (1999), starring Susan Sarandon and Natalie Portman.

Vera Wang

Fashion Designer
1949–

When Vera Wang became engaged to Arthur Becker in 1989, she knew just what kind of wedding dress she wanted. It had to be elegant, modern, and very sophisticated. She certainly did not want bows, ruffles, and yards of netting; after all Vera Wang was going to be forty years old on her wedding day. But her search for the perfect dress was not a happy one. Even at the top New York City fashion houses, everything seemed to be designed for little girls.

Of course Vera Wang was a tough customer. She had been senior fashion editor at the American edition of *Vogue* magazine for sixteen years and more recently a design director for Ralph Lauren. She knew clothes and she knew what looked good on her. When she could not find the dress of her dreams, she sketched a sleek satin hand-beaded gown and then paid a dressmaker $10,000 to turn her idea into reality. She was scarcely back from her honeymoon when she prepared to open the Vera Wang Bridal House on Madison Avenue in New York City. Today the name Vera Wang is synonymous with the most elegant bridal and evening gowns.

Vera Wang had no formal design training, but her years at *Vogue* and Ralph Lauren had given her a well-trained fashion eye. Wang also credits her mother, who loved high fashion and took her daughter on shopping trips with her to Paris and London, for her own good taste. Both her parents had grown up on mainland China and had escaped just before the Communist takeover. When Vera Wang was born in New York City, her father was already a wealthy oil executive who was able to give his children the best of everything. She attended exclusive private schools and studied at the American Ballet School, but her true passion was figure skating. She spent hours on the ice each day and, by her late teens, was a nationally ranked pairs skater. When she decided to attend Sarah Lawrence College, she gave up competitive skating.

Yet it was her intimate knowledge of skating that helped launch her career as a fashion designer. In 1992, just two years after opening her bridal house, Vera Wang was approached by the coach of top figure skater Nancy Kerrigan to design a dress for the next Olympics. At first Wang refused, mostly because she knew well the demands placed on a "nightmare of a bathing suit," as she called it. The tiny dress had to look as lovely as an evening gown yet its wearer needed to be able to do triple jumps without a rip, tear, or wrinkle. She finally did accept the challenge and created an elegant white-beaded costume that Nancy Kerrigan wore in the 1994 Olympics. Nancy Kerrigan's memorable silver medal performance, and her stunning outfit, were both noticed around the world. Many believed Nancy's shimmering elegance was at least in part due to Vera Wang.

Soon Vera Wang was asked to design gowns for movie stars and socialites, and her creations became commonplace on the runways of the Academy Awards and other prominent ceremonies.

Vera Wang takes an intellectual approach to designing, putting to use her graduate studies in art history and her years as a *Vogue* editor. She starts each new dress the way an architect designs a building, taking care with the "nuts and bolts," including how a skirt is draped or a sleeve mounted. Her finished products are like the figure skaters she admires—sleek and elegant with seemingly effortless grace. No one suspects the dedication and passion that have gone into each precise detail.

Gary Locke

Governor
1950–

There was nothing privileged about Gary Locke's childhood. He spent his first six years in a Seattle public housing project built for World War II veterans. One of five children, his father eventually bought a Chinese restaurant at Seattle's Pike Market, and the entire family worked there after school and on weekends. Through hard work, his father, James Locke, moved the family out of the projects. Taking the same path, Gary became an Eagle Scout, an honors student, and received a scholarship to attend Yale University.

Actually, James Locke was a tough act to follow even for a determined workaholic like Gary. James's father came to Washington around the turn of the century and worked as a house servant. He later moved back to China, but Gary's father returned to Washington and then enlisted in the army. He served under famed General Patton during World War II and landed on the beaches of Normandy, France, during the D-Day invasion. After the war, James Locke went to Hong Kong where he met and married his wife, Julie, before returning to Seattle.

Gary Locke studied political science at Yale and, three years later, received his law degree from Boston University. He then returned to Washington and became deputy prosecutor for King County, which includes Seattle. In that position he tried to win convictions of those accused of such serious crimes as robbery or murder.

When Gary Locke was elected to the Washington House of Representatives in 1982, he began to focus on the issues that interested him most. Believing that education was the pathway to success and that state government should help make it available to everyone, he worked to increase the amount of aid available to disadvantaged students wishing to go to college. Locke also wanted to improve children's health care and to work for important legislation for the environment.

He spent one term as chief executive of King County and then in 1996 he ran for governor. With his wife, Mona, a former news anchor, at his side he was an extremely appealing candidate. When he won the election he became the first Asian American governor. In November 2000 he was reelected to a second term.

Talk now centers on a possible run for the presidency. Even though Gary Locke stresses he has no particular presidential ambitions, Asian American supporters feel he is the perfect candidate. As they reason, one Asian candidate for the highest office, even if he is not successful, raises the visibility of all Asian candidates. Perhaps the pressure for him to at least try will be overwhelming.

Eugene H. Trinh

Physicist, Astronaut
1950–

On July 4, 1992, Eugene Trinh helped the United States celebrate its 216th birthday. He and the other members of the space shuttle *Columbia* crew set off sparklers and then sang a rousing version of the "Star Spangled Banner." For Dr. Trinh, the first Vietnamese American to fly on a U.S. spacecraft, it was, to say the least, a memorable occasion.

When Eugene Trinh was born in Saigon in 1950, Vietnam was called French Indochina and was engaged in a bloody war with France. (That war, which had begun in 1946, would end with the French leaving the country in 1954.) To escape the violence and social upheaval, the Trinh family moved to Paris in 1952.

Eugene Trinh attended French elementary schools where, right from the start, he distinguished himself in math and science. In 1968 he graduated from Paris's Lycée Michelet, one of the city's most respected high schools. New York City's Columbia University lured him away from Europe with the offer of a full scholarship.

Four years later, Trinh graduated from Columbia with a degree in mechanical engineering and applied physics. At Yale University he completed his doctoral degree in applied physics and then began his life's work with the U.S. space agency, NASA.

Dr. Trinh's research is in acoustics, which is the science of sound. An acoustical specialist tests the effects of sound and sound waves on various materials in different environments. For both NASA and the Jet Propulsion Laboratory in Pasadena, California, Trinh developed experiments that could be performed on space flights.

These experiments have involved testing high-temperature materials in both low-gravity and normal conditions. Of particular interest to Trinh's research are the effects of low gravity over time. The *Columbia* space shuttle's mission, which was to stay in orbit longer than any previous shuttle flight, provided him the perfect opportunity to test his research. He was named one of the mission's payload specialists.

While in orbit, Trinh performed experiments that tested what happens to fire in a weightless environment. One of his broad goals was to observe whether the low-gravity experience in outer space could offer scientists clues to the causes of Earth's serious environmental problems. The mission, which ended on July 10, was proclaimed a great success. In 1999 Eugene Trinh was named director of NASA's Microgravity Research Program.

Eugene Trinh and his wife, Yvette, a native of France, live in Culver City, California. When Trinh is not working at his lab in Pasadena, he likes to tinker around his house or play tennis in the warm California sun.

Amy Tan

Novelist
1952–

Several years ago, when Amy Tan asked her mother what life had been like in Shanghai, China, during World War II, Dora Tan said simply, "I wasn't affected." When Amy Tan pressed for more details, her mother told stories of Japanese bombing raids several times a week and how she and her family would run first to the city's east gate, then to the west gate, hoping the bombs would not fall on their heads. "But I thought you said you weren't affected," Amy answered. "I wasn't," her mother said. "I wasn't killed."

That difference between the American and Chinese perspectives on war, danger, and "being affected" became the subject of Amy Tan's second novel, *The Kitchen God's Wife*, published in 1991. This second book was anxiously awaited since Tan's first, *The Joy Luck Club*, published in 1989, had surprised everyone by becoming a best-seller and making its author an overnight literary star.

Amy Tan's parents came separately from China to the United States after World War II. They met in San Francisco, where they eventually married and raised three children. Like many Chinese parents raising children in America, the Tan's wanted their three children to take advantage of all the opportunities they themselves had missed. They urged them to study hard and fit into American society. Life seemed completely ordinary, Amy remembers, until 1967 when Amy's father and brother both died of cancer. Then Amy's mother told her two daughters something about herself that would change them forever.

Before coming to America, Dora Tan had been married and divorced. When she had fled Shanghai after the war, she had left behind three daughters. She had planned to bring them to the United States once she was settled, but when the Communists took over China in 1949, the girls were not allowed to leave. Soon after that, all communication between the citizens of China and the United States ceased, and Amy's mother lost track of her oldest children. This stunning news set Tan's literary imagination on fire.

In 1987 Mrs. Tan and her daughters were reunited in China. This joyous occasion proved to Amy that her ties to her lost sisters and to China were much stronger than she had ever imagined. How strongly she was affected by the new relationships in her life is evident in the book she published two years later.

The Joy Luck Club, based on Mrs. Tan's own experiences, is about four first-generation Chinese mothers and their "Americanized" second-generation daughters. The mothers, who meet often to drink tea and play a Chinese game called mah-jongg, talk about their Chinese pasts and their American children, who often seem like strangers to them. The daughters are embarrassed by their mothers who, they believe, wear "funny Chinese dresses with stand-up collars and silk-embroidered flowers." The misunderstandings continue until one of the club members dies and her own daughter takes her place in the Joy Luck Club. She then begins to understand the pain suffered by the older women and the changes they have had to make in their personal lives.

Since the publication of *The Joy Luck Club* and *The Kitchen God's Wife,* Amy Tan has published two more novels, *The Hundred Secret Senses* (1995) and *The Bonesetter's Daughter* (2000). She has also published two acclaimed stories for children, *The Chinese Siamese Cat* and *The Moon Lady.* Tan and her husband now divide their time between San Francisco and New York City.

Myung-Whun Chung

Musician, Music Director, Conductor
1953–

Controversy swirled around the opening of the new Opéra de la Bastille in Paris, France. For months, even years, before its scheduled first performance in the summer of 1989 nothing seemed to go right. The building—modern and glassy on one of Paris's most historic sites—cost more than $400 million, yet few found anything about it to praise.

About a year before the opening of the Opéra de la Bastille, the project's top administrator was fired. His replacement then fired the conductor who had been chosen to head the opera company. Then, in yet another risky move, the new conductor hired to lead the company into its most important season was a thirty-seven-year-old Korean-born American named Myung-Whun Chung.

Myung-Whun Chung could not speak French and did not have much experience conducting opera. He was a highly esteemed pianist and orchestral conductor, who had proven he could rise to tough challenges. But was he, the French public wondered, a miracle worker?

Myung-Whun Chung was born in Seoul, Korea, on January 22, 1953, the sixth of seven children of musically gifted parents. Music was so important to the Chungs that when, in the early 1950s, they had to flee the invading Communist-led forces of North Korea, their piano was one of the only family treasures they took with them during the escape.

At the age of seven, Myung-Whun Chung made his piano debut with the Seoul Philharmonic. He was not terribly nervous, though, because three of his sisters had played with the Seoul Philharmonic before him. Myung-Wha had played the cello, Kyung-Wha the violin, and Myung-So the flute.

When Myung-Whun's sister, Kyung-Wha Chung, won a scholarship to New York City's famed Juilliard School, the entire family moved to the United States. In 1961 the Chungs settled in Seattle, Washington. Kyung-Wha and Myung-Wha attended Juilliard in New York while Myung-Whun completed high school. Then he, too, moved to New York City to attend Juilliard. At Juilliard, Chung's focus shifted from piano playing to conducting. After graduation, however, he still was not sure whether his future lay with the piano or the conductor's baton.

During his years in New York, Myung-Whun Chung became a U.S. citizen and met Sunyol, the woman he later married. In 1978 he was named assistant conductor of the Los Angeles Symphony and within a few years became an associate conductor. He grew weary, though, of the additional duties of a music director, such as fund-raising and publicity. By the early 1980s, he was ready for a change. He and his wife moved to Europe so that he could conduct in different cities of the world.

Chung became the music director and principal conductor for the Radio Symphony Orchestra in Saarbrücken, West Germany, in 1984. A few years later he and Sunyol moved to Italy where he performed as a principal guest conductor. He also appeared with major orchestras in France, Britain, Israel, Germany, the Netherlands, and the United States.

By 1989 when Chung became the music director of the Opéra de la Bastille, his life had changed greatly from his carefree days in New York and Los Angeles. He and his wife were now the parents of three sons, and he was an experienced conductor and director. They welcomed the opportunity to live and work in Paris. Despite the Bastille Opéra's problems, the Chungs were looking forward to his new position.

Almost immediately Chung was thrown into the middle of enormous problems. The Opéra de la Bastille, whose construction was announced by French president François Mitterand in 1982, was to open in time for the 200th anniversary celebration of the start of the French Revolution, which occurred on July 14, 1789. This meant that Chung had only a few months to get things together. The new building was not yet complete. The opera that was to open the celebration had been changed, and the fast-approaching opera season had to be organized.

Chung's assignment was to create an opera company that would give up to 250 performances in one year and whose opening would mark a new beginning for France's place in the arts. Into this arena Chung strode confidently. A man of three continents—Korean by birth, American by citizenship, and European by current employment—he felt he was just the person for this challenge.

When the curtain finally rose on March 17, 1990, everything seemed ready. And when the curtain came down, everyone agreed that the performance of *Les Troyens* was nothing short of triumphant. The man whose mission had been compared to "taking command of the *Titanic* after it hit the iceberg" turned out to be a brilliant captain. All seemed confident the ship would sail!

Elaine Chao

Secretary of Labor
1953–

"I know what discrimination is," Elaine Chao, the first Asian American woman to be named a member of a president's cabinet, once told a reporter. Her family moved to the United States from Taiwan when Elaine, who did not speak English, was just eight. On her first day of school in New York City, she greeted her third grade teacher with a low bow of respect, just as she had been taught to do back in Taiwan. As she lowered her head, she heard her classmates burst into laughter. Fighting back tears of humiliation, she vowed not to let her insensitive classmates hold her back even a single day.

Fortunately, in order to move ahead in an unfriendly world, Elaine Chao had only to follow the example of her parents, who had fled Communist China for Taiwan just a few years before Elaine's birth. Her father had only been a merchant seaman in China, but in the relative freedom of Taiwan he was able to establish an international shipping business. When the family came to the United States, Mr. Chao was a wealthy man and able to give his own children all the educational advantages this country could offer.

Following high school, Elaine Chao attended Mount Holyoke College in Massachusetts and then Harvard Business School. With her master's degree in business administration, Elaine was ready to follow her father into business and finance. She worked for a time at the Bank of America in San Francisco.

In 1983 when Elaine was just thirty years old, she was named a White House Fellow. This fellowship allows those who work outside of government to be a part of the president's staff for one year. After her year in Washington, Elaine returned to banking, but her White House experience had changed her life forever. In 1989 she was named deputy secretary of transportation, becoming the highest-ranking Asian American ever in the executive branch of the government.

In 1991 President George Bush named Elaine Chao director of the Peace Corps, an organization that sends more than 6,000 volunteers to ninety-one countries. The next year she became president of United Way of America, the country's largest institution of private charitable giving. It was a tough position for any executive since her immediate predecessor had been accused of mismanaging funds and even stealing the agency's money. After these charges became public, donations to the United Way dropped dramatically. Chao's assignment was nothing less than rescuing a dying institution. As a practical and symbolic matter, she cut her own salary at the same time she slashed the agency's operating budget and laid off staff. Within a few years confidence in the United Way was restored.

Still, despite her sparkling successes, Elaine Chao's nomination by incoming President George W. Bush in January 2001 was controversial. Here was an Asian American who was opposed to both affirmative action and racial quotas. In her own defense she spoke of her service on Harvard University's alumni board and how she had witnessed firsthand the way racial quotas can work against Asians. Following Senate confirmation, she became the twenty-fourth secretary of labor on January 29, 2001.

Elaine Chao is one half of a successful Washington couple. Her husband is U.S. Senator Mitch McConnell of Kentucky, a prominent Republican. Despite her very American-style success story, Elaine Chao is very clear when she speaks of her Asian heritage. As much as she has gained from living in America, she believes this country has much to learn from Asians as well. Patience, hard work, strong family ties, and respect for others are qualities Elaine wishes Americans valued as much as Asians do. Ever since her first day of third grade, Elaine has tried to set an example all Americans might wish to follow.

Ang Lee

Film Director
1954–

When Ang Lee first left his parent's home in Taiwan for the United States, he believed he had become a family disgrace. Not only had he failed the entrance exam for a prestigious university in Taipei, but he had decided to become not a doctor or a businessman as his parents wished but an actor. After completing his required military service in Taiwan, Ang Lee boarded a plane for the long trip to the University of Illinois, where he planned to study theater. He knew his family was a little relieved to see him go.

Ang Lee had always loved American movies, and at the university, he gained an appreciation for European drama as well. He came to understand that one basic difference between Asian and Western theater is the way emotions are expressed. Asian actors usually try to hide emotion behind masks and grand physical gestures. In the plays of the great European dramatists, such as Shakespeare or Ibsen, deep feelings are pushed and pulled out of both the characters and the audience. Lee wanted to enter this territory as well. He imagined himself portraying the emotional lives of individual families, although on film instead of on the stage. After receiving his bachelor's degree from the University of Illinois, Ang Lee enrolled at the New York University Film School.

During his years at NYU Lee met and worked with other film students, including the young African American Spike Lee. After graduation Ang Lee moved into his own apartment and tried to become, in his words, "a well-connected New York filmmaker." Despite his training, he had trouble convincing film producers to let him direct his own work, and he struggled to earn a living. One day in 1983 he received a letter from his parents telling him that they would very soon make their first visit to New York. Worried that his father would, once again, be disappointed by his lack of success, Ang Lee decided to make their visit memorable in other ways. He called his college girlfriend, Jane Lin, who was just completing her doctoral degree at Illinois, and asked her to marry him during his parent's visit. Jane agreed and joined him a week later.

Lee's parents, however, were outraged at the last-minute wedding plans. After waiting in line at New York's City Hall, Ang and Jane stood before a justice of the peace who could not keep their names straight and rushed through the service. Afterward the four had lunch in a shabby Chinatown restaurant. Mr. Lee was deeply disappointed and left New York angrier than ever at his wayward son.

In fact father and son did not patch up their relationship until 1993, when Mr. Lee saw Ang's second film, *The Wedding Banquet*, at the Berlin Film Festival. Ang Lee had recreated his own offbeat New York City wedding in this film and, finally, even his father had to admit it was funny. *The*

Wedding Banquet, an international success, was followed the next year by *Eat Drink Man Woman.* Lee called this film, made in Taiwan and entirely in Mandarin Chinese, the last of his "Father Knows Best" trilogy. (The first, made in New York by a Taiwanese film company, is called *Pushing Hands.*)

Eat Drink Man Woman tells the story of a retired renowned chef, who is also the widowed father of three grown daughters. The father shows his love for his family by cooking elaborate meals. Not surprisingly, when his daughters do not stop their busy lives long enough to share his food he is deeply depressed. Ang Lee hired three full-time chefs to work on this film, and they prepared over a hundred Taiwanese and Chinese dishes.

Eat Drink Man Woman was even more successful than Ang Lee's first two films and finally this "New York filmmaker" was in demand to direct movies in English. In 1995 Ang was asked to make *Sense and Sensibility,* which would be based on the novel by Jane Austen written in the 1790s. The film was to be shot on location in England with an all-British cast. After Lee agreed to direct *Sense and Sensibility,* he admitted it was a risky venture for both the studio and for himself. Yet in some ways *Sense and Sensibility* was not so different from his earlier films, despite the time period, setting, and language. Both Jane Austen and Ang Lee are masters at creating closely observed scenes of love and family relationships.

Yet as Ang Lee's fame grew, his own family life changed little. He and Jane, a medical researcher, have raised their two sons in Westchester County, just outside of New York City. Ang made the 1997 film *The Ice Storm* in the New York area but, in 1998, he returned to Taiwan and mainland China to begin what would become his best-known film to date, *Crouching Tiger, Hidden Dragon.* A martial-arts fantasy with two tender love stories at its heart, it finally made Ang Lee one of the world's best-known directors. He won the Academy Award for Best Director in 2000 and in 2001, *Time* magazine named him "America's Best Director."

Yo-Yo Ma

Cellist
1955–

"When I give a concert, I like to think that I'm welcoming someone to my home," Yo-Yo Ma said once before going on stage at one of Europe's great concert halls. "I've lived with the music a long time; it's an old friend, and I want to say, 'Let's all participate.'"[24]

And yet as he takes up the cello and begins to play, he seems to slip into another world, deep within the sound of the music. Not content to merely read the page and produce the sounds, Yo-Yo Ma actually listens to the music as he plays. He closes his eyes and moves his head back as though he were trying to move as far away from his cello as possible. His breath, his face, his entire body seem to change, ready to do whatever the music asks.

His intense concentration is one of the many things he learned, at least in part, from his father, Hiao-Tsiun Ma. While a respected professor of music at China's Nanjing University during the 1930s, Hiao-Tsiun Ma became concerned about the political conditions in his native country and decided to move to Paris. One of his students, a gifted singer named Marina, followed. The two were married in 1949. In 1951 a daughter, Yeou-Cheng, was born and on October 7, 1955, a son, Yo-Yo (Yo means "friendship" in Mandarin Chinese).

According to Yo-Yo Ma, his father looked upon teaching not so much as a profession, but as a way of life. Mr. Ma tutored his two children in history, Chinese literature, and calligraphy. Each child also played an instrument at a very early age: Yeou-Cheng the violin and Yo-Yo the cello.

Mr. Ma's method for teaching young children was simple. He gave them very short assignments, which were to be learned thoroughly. Every day, for example, four-year-old Yo-Yo Ma was expected to memorize two measures of Bach. Day by day, two measures at a time, Yo-Yo learned to understand the pattern of Bach and slowly began to understand musical structure.

As he grew older and was expected to learn complicated pieces quickly, he applied the basic principle learned from his father. Break the problem up into four parts, Hiao-Tsiun Ma would teach, then approach each without fear. After the parts are completed, put them all back together, and you will have mastered something that at first seemed too complex.

Under his father's guidance, Yo-Yo Ma progressed so rapidly that at the age of five he gave his first public concert at the University of Paris. Then in 1962, Mr. Ma's brother in New York asked for help in a family emergency. The entire family left Paris for New York, fully intending to return after six months. In fact, their stay in America became permanent.

Yo-Yo Ma's musical gifts were immediately noticed in New York, and he began studying with the most distinguished cellists. Throughout his teens he performed with orchestras around the world. At home in New York, though, the family was in turmoil as Mr. Ma tried to enforce strict Chinese values upon his newly Americanized son. "My home life was totally structured," he remembered. "Because I couldn't rebel there, I did so at school."

All of a sudden the perfect student began missing classes and snapping back at his teachers. The genius was becoming lazy and undisciplined. At the Juilliard School, his cello teacher advised he see a psychiatrist. Yo-Yo Ma was confused about what kind of a person he would become. He knew he wanted to be a great musician, but he also wanted to learn as much about art, literature, science, and life as possible.

Yo-Yo Ma enrolled at Harvard University, combining a rigorous liberal arts program with a career as a concert cellist. In between classes and exams, he jetted off to world capitals to perform as a soloist with great orchestras. As the number of concert engagements grew, pressures on his academic work became overwhelming. Ma seriously considered dropping out of Harvard, but his father stepped in and counseled his son to limit his concert engagements and finish his college education.

Early in his career, Yo-Yo Ma recorded Johann Sebastian Bach's "Suites for Unaccompanied Cello," and this remains one of his best-known works. In addition to appearing as a solo performer in concert halls around the world, he has often collaborated with the esteemed pianist Emmanuel Ax. In recent years Yo-Yo Ma has gone beyond the classical repertoire and recorded albums with jazz, country, and Latin musicians. He has also performed on the sound track of the award-winning Chinese language film, *Crouching Tiger, Hidden Dragon*. Yo-Yo Ma, his wife, Jill, and their two children live in the Boston area.

Gish Jen

Writer
1955–

"Typical American" is a term with at least two meanings. To some it means a fair-haired, native-born, English-speaking U.S. citizen—a definition that, of course, leaves out most Americans. At another level, as author Gish Jen points out, it can mean the things immigrants do not like about Americans. Her Chinese parents, for example, warned her not to imitate the loud, rude, and greedy behavior of some Americans. With so many layers of meaning, Gish Jen thought *Typical American* (1991) was the perfect title for her first novel.

In at least one important way, the immigrant experience of Gish Jen's parents was definitely not typical. Her mother and father had been sent to the United States by the Chinese government just after World War II to learn new skills they could use to help rebuild their war-torn country. When the Communists took over China in 1949, the Jens were not allowed to return. "Just think," Gish Jen says, "if you went to China to study for a year and were forced to remain there—no money, no knowledge of language, and a complete rupture from family and friends."

The conflict between parents, whose hearts and souls are in China, and their children, who want to be accepted by their American classmates, appears again and again in Chinese American literature. Since traditionally the authority of one's father and mother is absolute in China, clashes between Chinese parents and their American children can be especially tense. ("Typical American just-want-to-be-the-center-of-things," or "Typical American don't-know-how-to-get-along," snips Helen, the mother in *Typical American.*) Chinese-American children, for their part, find it hard—if not impossible—to live in two cultures at the same time.

The Jen family eventually settled in the prosperous New York suburb of Scarsdale. They gave their oldest daughter the English name of Lillian, but while she was in high school she decided such an old-fashioned name was not for her. Instead she took the last name of the famous American silent film actress, Lillian Gish.

Gish Jen's parents wanted her to be a doctor and were happy when she was admitted to Harvard. While in college, however, she decided to major in English and hoped to one day become a writer. Her parents did not approve. Nor were they pleased when Gish Jen moved to Colorado and became a ski bum. From the ski slopes of the Rockies, she went to China and taught English for a year. "My year in China," she remembered, "helped me understand certain parts of my parents. For example, the Chinese never question authority. . . . They take great pains to go around it."[25]

Finally Gish Jen was able to see how upsetting her own behavior had been for her mother and father. She saw her rebellion through their eyes. As she edged toward understanding her parents and their Chinese past, she also became a writer who could truly put herself in another's place.

Early in *Typical American,* Helen—based on Jen's own mother—realizes that her stay in America is going to last a long time. Depressed over circumstances beyond her control, she knows she will soon have to begin living in, rather than just visiting, America: "For the first few months, she could hardly sit without thinking how she might be wearing out her irreplaceable [Chinese] clothes. How careful she had to be! . . . Helen walked as little and as lightly as she could, sparing her shoes that they might last until the Nationalists saved the country and she could go home again."[26]

Typical American, which took Gish Jen four years to write, was published in 1991 and nominated for the American Book Award. It was followed in 1996 by *Mona in the Promised Land,* a novel about a Chinese girl from the New York suburbs who shocks her parents by converting to Judaism. In 1999 Gish Jen published a collection of short stories called *Who's Irish: Stories Today.* Gish Jen and her husband, David O'Connor, live in Cambridge, Massachusetts, with their two children, Luke and Paloma.

David Henry Hwang

Playwright
1957–

"Never trust appearances" is the message of David Henry Hwang's plays. People may look Asian or African, masculine or feminine, but that does not mean you know who they really are. The outcome of Hwang's award-winning play *M. Butterfly*, which is about a French diplomat's love for a Chinese actress, startled many audiences with this profound idea.

Born in Los Angeles, David Hwang grew up in a wealthy suburb. His father, a native of Shanghai, China, was the president of a bank in Los Angeles's Chinatown. Both his parents had come to the United States from China during the 1940s, yet despite being a first-generation citizen, Hwang's upbringing was so all-American, he rarely thought about being Asian. He knew he was Chinese, he once said, but it seemed a minor detail, like the color of his hair.

Hwang's strongest awareness of his heritage came from his grandmother's "talk-stories," which were like tall tales about the family's history in China. When he was twelve years old, he started to write these stories down. Later he was deeply affected by the writings of fellow Chinese American Maxine Hong Kingston, who worked her own mother's talk-stories into an acclaimed book, *The Woman Warrior*. David began to work his grandmother's stories into his writing as well.

After graduating from a Los Angeles area prep school, David Henry Hwang attended Stanford University, where he majored in English and learned to love the theater. At Stanford he also tried his hand at playwriting, which "seemed to me the most magical form. . . . I knew I wanted to write things, to create worlds and then see the worlds right in front of me."

His first play, written while still a student, was called *F.O.B.*—which he used as an acronym for "fresh off the boat," an unflattering name for a new arrival to America. The play is about the clash between a "fresh-off-the-boat" Chinese man and his American cousin. The play was well received in San Francisco and eventually was staged in New York City, where it won an Obie Award for the best off-Broadway play of the 1980–81 season.

While a student at the Yale School of Drama, David wrote a play about the Chinese immigrants who built the first transcontinental railroad. He had read about these nineteenth-century workers and wanted to do away with the image of them as "little coolies," indistinguishable one from the other. *The Dance and the Railroad* tells of two men who, during a long labor strike, practice the complicated dance movements of the Chinese opera. The two workers share a dream of one day performing with the Beijing Opera.

Several years after a successful New York run of *The Dance and the Railroad*, David Henry Hwang's play *M. Butterfly* was mounted on the New

York stage. The story is based on the true-life case of a French diplomat in love beyond reason with a Chinese actress. The Frenchman is eventually found guilty of passing state secrets to his mistress, who turns out to be not only a Chinese intelligence agent but a man. The unfortunate Frenchman claims he knew nothing about the actress's sexual identity or true profession. But how? The playwright explores the way strong emotions, and prejudices, make people fool themselves.

Since *M. Butterfly*'s opening in 1988, it has won several major awards, including a Tony Award for the best Broadway play of the year, and has played to packed theaters around the world. It was also a successful movie. David Henry Hwang received more awards for his 1998 play *Golden Gate*. Today he lives in New York City, where he writes for television, film, and theater. He is currently working on a new version of the 1950s musical *Flower Drum Song*.

Maya Ying Lin

Architect, Sculptor
1959–

When Maya Lin was twenty-one and a senior at Yale University, she entered a national contest to design a monument honoring the veterans of the Vietnam War. The site of the future monument was impressive: 2 acres in Washington, D.C., near the Lincoln Memorial and the Washington Monument. Maya Lin was only in grade school during the height of the war and was not personally affected, but she knew it was still an emotional issue for many Americans. She understood, too, that the purpose of the memorial was to soothe some of the anger and pain of the Vietnam years.

Maya Lin submitted a pastel drawing of a simple black V-shaped wall tucked into the side of a small hill. On the wall's black granite surface were to be carved the names of the 58,229 men and women who died during the war or were still missing. There were 1,420 other contest entries, but in the end, the panel of judges unanimously agreed that Maya Lin's spare design was the most powerful. Just after graduating from Yale in 1981, Lin left for Washington to oversee construction of the Vietnam Wall.

The Vietnam Veterans Memorial opened on Veteran's Day 1982. Since then millions of people have stood before the names. They come to reflect and cry and touch the cold black granite. The presence of so many people makes the wall truly a living memorial to the war's dead. "To me, it's a very simple notion," Maya Lin told a reporter. "You cannot ever forget that war is not just a victory or loss. It's really about individual lives."

Maya Ying Lin was born in Athens, Ohio, in 1959. Her parents had fled Shanghai, China, in the late 1940s. After arriving in the United States, they both accepted teaching positions at Ohio University. Mr. Lin was the university's dean of fine arts until his death in 1989. Her mother still teaches English and Asian literature.

Maya Lin attended Yale University as both an undergraduate and, later, as a graduate student in architecture. Unlike most students who worry about finding the right job after graduation, Lin was well established in her field when she left school. Indeed, the Vietnam Veterans' Memorial had brought her international recognition.

After she completed work on the memorial, Maya Lin settled into a career as an architect and sculptor. She had decided not to design any more public monuments but changed her mind after receiving a call in 1988 from the Southern Poverty Law Center in Montgomery, Alabama. The center's directors wanted to build a civil rights memorial that would occupy the plaza in front of their headquarters in Montgomery.

Maya Lin spent months studying the civil rights movement and, as she said, "waiting for a form to show up." Finally, one day she came across a biblical phrase that was used in two speeches given by Martin Luther King Jr.: "We will not be satisfied until justice rolls down like waters and righteousness like a mighty stream." Reading those words, Lin knew that water would be a part of the monument. She decided to make a timeline of the movement's major events, including the killings of forty men, women, and children, and cover the words with a fine layer of water. As with the Vietnam Memorial, visitors are invited to touch the carved granite and, in a sense, join hands with the dead. The Civil Rights Memorial was dedicated in the fall of 1989.

Since then Maya Lin has completed a few other public monuments, including one at Yale University. She was the subject of a 1994 film, *Maya Lin: A Strong Clear Vision*, which won an Academy Award for best documentary. In 2000 she published an autobiography called *Boundaries,* in which she explores the line between art and architecture, which she crosses many times in her own work. Today Maya Lin lives in New York City with her husband and two daughters.

Greg Louganis

Olympic Diver
1960–

After three Olympics and more than ten World Championships, it had come down to one dive. Greg Louganis had already completed nine out of ten dives and was in second place in the platform competition of the 1988 Summer Olympics. As he walked up the ladder to the platform, he tried not to look at Xiong Ni, the fourteen-year-old Chinese boy who was in first place, or to think that this was his last Olympic dive and that it had to be nothing short of perfect. Instead, he pictured the dive in his mind. He saw himself at the edge of the concrete, his arms rising like the wings of a bird.

Minutes later, as Greg Louganis climbed out of the pool, the computer flashed his score. The audience roared as they realized this great champion had won another gold medal, becoming the first man in history to win two gold medals in back-to-back Olympics. Then the man whom one journalist described as "running on pure courage" broke down crying.

"Pure courage" was something Louganis had drawn on many times during his troubled youth. His parents—a handsome, dark Samoan father and a blond, blue-eyed mother—were fifteen when he was born. They decided to give their son up for adoption. His new parents, Peter and Frances Louganis of San Diego, provided a loving home for Greg and Despina, a girl who had been adopted earlier.

School, however, was a constant source of misery for Louganis. He was teased about his dark features and always felt he was an outsider. To make matters worse, he had trouble learning to read. He struggled to make sense out of words that appeared to be just a jumble of letters. His teachers did not know that his problem had a name—dyslexia.

As an athlete, however, Greg Louganis was able to outperform anyone. He excelled at gymnastics and began diving at age nine. As soon as he joined his town's competitive diving team, he became its best diver. By eleven, he was chosen for the Junior Olympics held in Colorado. As he entered junior high he was already thought to be one of America's best young divers.

What made Greg Louganis such a good diver? For one, his legs were unusually strong. On a springboard he could jump higher than others, and with the extra height, he could stay in the air longer. His dives never looked rushed. Greg also had superb concentration, which allowed him to clear his head and focus on one dive at a time.

Back at school, however, no one cared much about his diving skills. As he tried desperately to make friends, he got in with the "wrong crowd." His mother and father became alarmed, especially since he seemed to be losing interest in diving.

The Louganises contacted Dr. Sammy Lee, a former Olympic champion who often coached promising young divers. (His story can be found earlier in this book.) Dr. Lee saw that Greg's talent was truly extraordinary and offered to become both his coach and guardian.

Dr. Lee was able to communicate with Greg Louganis as few others could. He, too, had been called names because of his Asian ancestry. Dr. Lee's parents, however, who had both been born in Korea, had taught him that when others look down at you, you must work doubly hard.

With Dr. Lee's guidance Louganis prepared himself for world competition. At sixteen he won a silver medal at the 1976 Olympics in Montreal. By 1978 Greg had won the first of many world titles and he had moved on to a new coach, Ron O'Brien.

In 1980 the United States did not compete in the Olympic Games held in Moscow. Four years later in Los Angeles, Greg Louganis was cheered on by hometown crowds and won two gold medals. He truly became one of America's heroes.

No one really thought, however, that he would do it again—not even Greg himself. At first he did not think he would compete in the 1988 Summer Games in Seoul, Korea. He had acted in a movie, performed with a professional dance company, and begun to believe there was life outside of a swimming pool. But as the Olympic year approached, he again felt the pull of competition.

After his stunning double victory in Seoul, he was elevated to a position among the true heroes of sport. As he neared thirty, he retired from diving competitions. In an interview with journalist Barbara Walters in 1995, Greg told a television audience that he was gay and had tested positive for HIV and AIDS. That same year he published a book about his experience called *Breaking the Surface* and toured the country telling large crowds, "You need to love yourself enough to protect yourself."

Jerry Yang

Internet Entrepreneur
1968–

Jerry Yang likes to say that his life is Yahoo! and Yahoo! is his life. Yahoo!, the first company to provide Internet users a way to navigate the World Wide Web, began at the Stanford University office Jerry shared with fellow engineering student David Filo. During several months in the early 1990s, it must have indeed seemed to Yang that there was not much more to his life than that small office, its computers, the Web, and the empty pizza boxes piled in the corner. But, of course, there was.

Born in Taiwan, Jerry Yang was only two when his father died. His mother continued teaching English literature and drama until, when Jerry was ten, she decided to move to San Jose, California. Jerry knew almost no English when he entered the fourth grade. Yet he was talented with numbers and abstract concepts and so, following his mother's example of hard work and discipline, he mastered all his schoolwork. At eighteen he enrolled at Stanford University in nearby Palo Alto.

On a Stanford program in Japan, Jerry Yang became friends with David Filo, a fellow electrical engineering student. When they returned to the Stanford campus, they decided to share an office. The professor they both studied under left the country for several months that school year, and Yang and Filo allowed themselves to use the university computing system to "play around." What they wanted to do most of all was set sail on the World Wide Web.

They began compiling a list of their favorite Web sites. In 1994 Jerry Wang posted what he called "Jerry's Guide to the World Wide Web," mostly so his own friends could find the best (and coolest, as he called them) sites. As the list grew, Yang and Filo began breaking it up into categories. Eventually they called their directory Yahoo!, a name they were drawn to because of its playful reference to the Wild West. It was also easy to remember. By the end of 1994 Web users were accessing Yahoo! a million times a day.

As the site grew, Stanford began to have reservations about allowing the two graduate students to continue using the university's computer network. This was just the nudge they needed to begin thinking of their just-for-fun project as a real business venture. Even though they had never received any money for Yahoo!, they decided to leave Stanford and rent office space in the nearby town of Mountain View.

Yet turning Yahoo! into a moneymaking business was no small feat. Since it was supposed to be a free online service, how could they collect money? The first challenge was to find venture capitalists, those who would be willing to give them money to start the business, and so they invited bankers and investors into their new offices. Yet when the venture capitalists arrived wearing business suits and carrying briefcases, they often felt they were in David and Jerry's dorm room, not a real office. The two often looked as though they had not slept or changed their clothes in days—which, in fact, they often had not. Potential investors stumbled over dirty laundry and the leftovers of take-out meals on their way to the computer terminals.

Once, however, they learned about Yahoo! they were more than willing to invest. In late 1995 Yahoo! began selling online space to advertisers. In 1996 the company went public, meaning shares were offered for sale on the New York Stock Exchange. On the first day of trading the market value of this so-called graduate school project was $848 million, more than anyone dared hope.

Helping their company grow has occupied most of the free time of the two Chief Yahoos, as they like to call themselves. Yahoo! is not even ten years old and remains a leader in this very new and competitive field. Jerry Yang, who now likes to travel the world giving speeches about his company, owns a luxury home and has a staff to make his meals and keep his clothes clean. Still, his devotion to Yahoo! has not wavered since the days when he and David Filo were squeezed into their tiny Stanford office, just playing around.

Midori

Violinist
1971–

Midori was not quite ten when, in 1981, she was invited to perform at the Aspen Music Festival before an audience of fellow musicians. As she took center stage, many wondered how such a tiny girl could even hold a violin, much less play one. The great violinist Pinchas Zukerman recalled:

> I was sitting on a chair, and I was as tall as she was standing. She tuned, she bowed to the audience, she bowed to me, she bowed to the pianist—and then she played the Bartók concerto. . . . I sat there and tears started coming down my cheeks. . . . I was absolutely stunned. I turned to the audience and said, "Ladies and gentlemen, I don't know about you, but I've just witnessed a miracle.[27]

Born in Osaka, Japan, in 1971, Midori Goto began violin lessons shortly after her third birthday. Even before that, however, music was part of her life. She often waited in auditoriums while her mother, a concert violinist and teacher named Setsu Goto, gave classes and rehearsed. Midori's mother knew early on that her young daughter was deeply sensitive to music.

In 1982, just shy of Midori's eleventh birthday, Setsu Goto decided to leave Japan and enroll her daughter at the Juilliard School in New York City. While studying music at Juilliard, Midori also attended the Professional Children's School, a unique college preparatory school for children in the arts. It was at the Children's School that she learned English and received her academic education.

The adjustment to American culture for the Goto family was difficult, yet they were willing to make the necessary sacrifices for Midori's promising career. Her leap to the ranks of the world's great violinists seemed only a few years away.

By the time Midori was sixteen and still a student at Juilliard, she began appearing with orchestras in packed concert halls around the world. Audiences were thrilled with this tiny girl and her huge talent. Yet her mother and manager agreed Midori's career should not take off too fast. Believing that Midori needed more time to learn and mature, they decided to put off her solo debut.

In 1987 Midori made the controversial decision to leave the Juilliard School and prepare for her professional recital debut. Although she remained at the Professional Children's School, from which she graduated in 1990, leaving the Juilliard School allowed Midori the time she needed to prepare for her debut and accept invitations to perform with the world's great orchestras.

When the time came for Midori's debut, she chose New York's Carnegie Hall where so many great violinists, such as Jascha Heifetz and Yehudi

Menuhin, had made their starts while still quite young. Midori knew that to be forever compared with the greats, her recital would need to be perfect.

The recital date was set for October 25, 1990—just a few days after her nineteenth birthday. Despite the pressure, Midori was poised and confident. After all, Midori had been preparing for this moment since the time she first played her tiny violin for her mother. There was no way she was going to ruin the most important night of her life.

Carnegie Hall was sold out. Representatives from the Sony Corporation were there to make both a videotape and compact disc, yet Midori was cool and calm. Part of the reason, Midori explained, is that onstage she is truly at home. "I feel so comfortable onstage; I feel safest. The best part of giving concerts is just being out there and playing, nothing else." When the evening was over, critics pronounced the recital a "triumph."

Today Midori is in such demand as a soloist that she could be touring full time—if she wanted. Instead, she devotes a considerable portion of her time to Midori and Friends, a foundation that brings music to under-priviledged schoolchildren in New York City. Midori loves nothing more than sharing her passion for music, which she believes has the power to change people's lives.

Kristi Yamaguchi

Figure Skater
1971–

Kristi Yamaguchi and her coach hoped the Winter Olympics in Albertville, France, would prepare the young skater for the *next* Olympics just two years away in Norway. (Both the Summer and Winter Games used to be held once every four years in the same year, but the 1992 games in Albertville were followed by the 1994 Winter games in Lillehammer as a "catch up" year so the the Winter and Summer Olympics could then be held every alternating two years.) After all, Kristi had mostly been known as a pairs skater and had only made the switch to singles competition a few years earlier. But Yamaguchi rose to this very high-pressured occasion and became the

Ladies Singles Champion, winning over not only her loyal fans in America but also the entire world.

Kristi Yamaguchi was born in Fremont, California, in 1971. Her parents, Carole and Jim Yamaguchi, are third-generation Japanese Americans. Yet even though their families have lived in the United States since the early 1900s, they bear the scars of anti-Japanese discrimination. Carole Yamaguchi was born during World War II in a Colorado internment camp, where her family had been sent after the Japanese attack on Pearl Harbor in 1941. Like many Japanese Americans living in California at the time, her parents lost their home and business when they were imprisoned. Jim Yamaguchi's story was similar. Yet neither of Kristi's parents liked to dwell on their hardships. Instead they preferred to encourage their children's very American love of the outdoors and, especially, sports.

Kristi Yamaguchi began skating at age six and, from the start, was considered a natural on ice. By the time she was eight she had already begun working with a prominent coach, Christy Kjarsgaard. Just a few years after that she and her pairs partner, Rudi Galindo, began to enter national and international competitions. In 1986 Kristi and Rudi became the U.S. Pairs Champions. That same year Kristi also entered the singles competition and placed fourth.

In 1989 Kristi Yamaguchi became the first woman to compete in both the singles and pairs events at the World Championships. She had already placed first in pairs and second in singles during the U.S. Nationals earlier that year. She was disappointed, however, to be only fifth in pairs and sixth in singles at the World Championships and vowed to do better.

A day after her high school graduation Yamaguchi moved to Edmonton, Canada, where Christy Kjarsgaard now lived. She decided to devote herself entirely to singles training and set her goal as nothing short of becoming the world's top female skater. Her nearly legendary drive and work ethic helped her achieve her goal sooner than even her coach had hoped. She won the gold medal at the 1991 World Championships in Munich, Germany.

Kristi Yamaguchi was ecstatic with her victory, feeling that now everyone had to believe she could win Olympic gold. In Albertville, in 1992, she charmed the world with her bright smile and confident skating. With her stunning victory, she became the first American woman to win the gold medal in figure skating since Dorothy Hamill had done it sixteen years before in 1976. And just to make sure no one underestimated her again, Kristi Yamaguchi again won the World Championships a month later in Oakland, California.

Kristi became a professional skater later in 1992. Her poise and charm have continued to make her one of America's most popular athletes. She has repeatedly been named the World Pro Figure Skating Champion and, in 1999, she was inducted into the World Figure Skating Hall of Fame. In July 2000 Kristi Yamaguchi married professional hockey player Bret Hedican.

Michael Chang

Tennis Player
1972–

"These two weeks are going to stay with me the rest of my life," said Michael Chang after winning the French Open tennis tournament in June 1989. He was only seventeen and had just become both the youngest male ever to win one of the four Grand Slam tournaments and the first American to win the French Open in more than forty years.

Michael Chang was used to being the "youngest ever." At fifteen he was the youngest to win a pro tournament, then the youngest male to win a singles match at the U.S. Open. The following year he became the youngest ever to play on the legendary Center Court at Wimbledon, near London, England. So winning a Grand Slam tournament at seventeen seemed right on schedule.

Michael Chang was born on February 22, 1972. Joe Chang, Michael's father, had himself just taken up the game of tennis and was so enthusiastic about it he wanted his whole family to play. At a very early age he began preparing his son for tennis. Michael Chang played his first tennis match at age six and won his first tournament a year later.

Tennis remained a family affair as Michael Chang moved quickly through the ranks of the top junior players. The family moved from Minnesota to Placentia, California, so that Michael Chang could play year-round. Never one to do anything halfway, Joe Chang worked full time as a chemist and continued as his son's primary coach. An extremely organized man, Mr. Chang used training data plus his own readings and observations to plot out Michael's entire career.

In 1988 Michael Chang, an honors student at Placentia High School, scored well enough on the high school proficiency exam to graduate two years early. That same year, just as his father had planned, Chang made his professional tennis debut. Betty Chang left her job as a research chemist in order to travel on the pro tour with her son. She did his laundry, cooked his favorite Chinese meals, and saw to it that on the day following each tournament he was able to pursue his second favorite sport—fishing.

Michael Chang is, in many ways, an unlikely sports champion. Quiet, reflective, "just a nice guy," as many have called him, he likes to spend his spare time browsing in bookstores or enjoying the peace and quiet of nature. "Just being out there is comforting," is the way Chang describes his love of fishing.

More often, however, being "out there" means facing high-pressure situations in front of thousands of tennis fans. Since he won the French Open, neither the public nor the press have wanted to leave Michael Chang in peace. His love for the game of tennis has never wavered, but the distractions of being a celebrity have made for rough patches in his career. Just after winning the French Open, he hoped to settle comfortably in the ranks of the world's top tennis players. Instead, he moved up and down the rankings and often lost tournaments he was expected to win.

Michael Chang has found comfort in his Christian faith, which he shares with his entire family. He has tried to remember that he never wanted to be judged solely on his athletic ability. Instead he hopes his determination, hard work, and sense of responsibility will make him a role model to young sports fans. Michael Chang has been ranked as high as number two in the world in men's tennis. Just as important, however, was the day in 1995 when he was named by the newspaper *USA Today* as one of the world's most caring athletes.

Vietnamese Boat People

1970s

The Vietnam War ended when Communist forces conquered South Vietnam, Laos, and Cambodia in 1975. A new drama then began as the people of the defeated nations struggled to free themselves from harsh Communist rule. Some people fled to the jungles and joined armed resistance groups. Others chose to abandon their homelands altogether and emigrate elsewhere.

Beginning in the mid-1970s, hundreds of thousands of people fled South Vietnam. These desperate refugees came from all walks of life and included government officials, doctors, merchants, and ordinary laborers. Most people tried to escape with their entire families. Unfortunately, many did not make it out alive.

The escape route chosen by most was extremely perilous—by boat over the South China Sea. Vietnamese shores were carefully guarded against such

Vietnamese refugees crowd a boat as they make their escape from South Vietnam.

escapes, so those who actually succeeded did so with careful planning and a lot of luck. One man, a teacher named Phuong Hoang, bought a small fishing boat with a friend. For an entire year they posed as fishermen so they could learn how to navigate on the open sea. Phuong did not even reveal his escape plan to his family. Schoolteachers were known to be notorious government informers, and he feared that his children might innocently let news of the plan slip out in school. Being discovered could have serious consequences.

In 1976 Hoang finally managed to escape. He and his friend told their families to dress in swimsuits for a day of fun on the boat. Since they carried no luggage or extra supplies, the police were not suspicious. Once everyone was aboard, Hoang turned on the engine and sped from the shore as fast as he could. The eight people spent four fearful days on the open water. Dozens of ships passed, ignoring their SOS signals. Finally, after a journey of more than 900 miles (1,450 km), they were rescued by an Italian oil tanker and then transported to Saudi Arabia, from which they fled to Canada and to freedom.

Phuong Hoang's story is one of incredible luck. Many thousands were not so fortunate. They rode rickety boats that sank at sea or were set upon by pirates who robbed and raped them. Many died of hunger, dehydration, or exposure to the sun. Some escapees were detained by border guards before leaving Vietnam. Many of those who were lucky enough to escape and arrive at safe harbors in Indonesia, the Philippines, Taiwan, and Hong Kong were denied entry into the countries because of immigration quotas. Many refugees intentionally sank their boats upon arrival so the authorities could not send them back. By 1979 government policies began to change, and more refugees were allowed to emigrate to the West.

Most of the people who fled Vietnam hoped to make the United States their final destination. Because of U.S. quota restrictions, however, many were not accepted. As late as 1977, only 300 Asian immigrants were allowed into the United States every month. After 1977 quotas were increased—with restrictions, however. Immigrants had to be close relatives of U.S. citizens, former top officials of the defeated South Vietnamese government, or people who had collaborated with the United States during the war.

Once in the United States, even rich, important, and highly educated immigrants had to start careers in low-level, low-paying jobs. For a decade former South Vietnamese prime minister Nguyen Cao Ky lived quietly in Louisiana trying to run a liquor store and then a fishing business. After declaring bankruptcy, he moved near Los Angeles, California, where he lives with a sister in a Vietnamese community. Since relocating to California, he

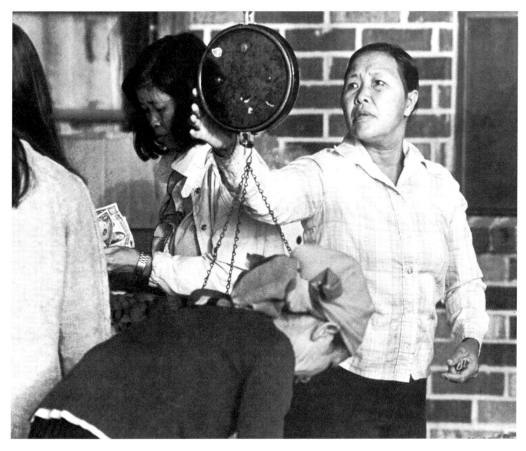

A busy market in the Michoud area of New Orleans where many Vietnamese have settled.

has been publicly advocating diplomatic and economic pressure on the Hanoi government to bring about democracy and freedom in Vietnam.

Adapting to the climate and customs of America has been difficult for Vietnamese immigrants. They have had to learn a new language while earning a living and adjusting to values that are very different from their own. Many feel that the very fabric of the Vietnamese family is being torn apart. Parents desperately cling to traditional values while their children rebel against them.

For example, in Vietnam most marriages are arranged by the parents when their children are very young, but in America adult children wish to choose their own husbands and wives. In Vietnam, families live in close proximity to each other; but in America many adult children often move far from their families and visit their parents infrequently, if at all.

Like many other immigrant communities that struggle to survive in America, the Vietnamese must cope with corruption, crime, and violence. In August 1979 a dispute between immigrant Vietnamese fishermen and residents of Seadrift, Texas, turned ugly when an American fisherman was killed and several Vietnamese fishing boats were firebombed in retaliation. In the 1980s Vietnamese street gangs were caught extorting money from local businesses and harassing ordinary citizens.

As first- and second-generation Vietnamese Americans join mainstream America, however, there are strong signs that life will improve for them. In urban communities such as Little Saigon, a bustling section of Orange County, California, young and old Vietnamese Americans succeed in American jobs yet still maintain their traditional customs. In education, more and more Vietnamese students compete at the highest levels.

Although more than a half-million refugees have emigrated to the United States since the end of the Vietnam War, many more still wait to come. The strict Communist regime in Vietnam continues to make life difficult. As the immigration waiting lists grow, people still attempt dangerous escapes from their homeland.

Hmong Refugees

1970s

At an early age Hmong girls are taught the art of *pa ndau*, a dazzling, intricate type of embroidery. In traditional Hmong culture, a girl's skill at pa ndau determines the wealth of her future husband. Since 1975, however, when the Hmong were forced to flee their mountainous homeland in Laos, Hmong women have used their embroidery to narrate their people's sad story. Their delicate stitchery shows the Hmong running from Vietnamese soldiers, crossing the Mekong River, and walking hundreds of miles to a refugee camp in Thailand. The final scene is of the long voyage to the United States.

The Hmong are tribal mountain dwellers from northern Laos, a small Southeast Asian country sandwiched between Vietnam and Thailand, with Cambodia and China as southern and northern neighbors, respectively. During the Vietnam War many Hmong men were employed by the U.S. Army as guerrilla fighters.

A customer buys produce at a small farmers' market run mostly by Hmong farmers in Minneapolis, Minnesota.

When the war ended with the defeat of the U.S.-backed forces, the Hmong were forced to flee Laos, which had been taken over by the Vietnamese Communists. Many Hmong were killed by Vietnamese soldiers, others were chased from their homes and walked hundreds of miles through jungles to a refugee camp in Thailand. From there, many began the long voyage across the Pacific. Today there are nearly 160,000 Hmong living in the United States—most live in California, Minnesota, and Wisconsin.

Refugees fleeing war and oppression have been seeking a safe haven in the United States for hundreds of years. Refugee workers, specially trained to help new arrivals find their way in a completely unfamiliar culture, have found that resettling the Hmong is extremely difficult. According to one resettlement worker, the American way of life is so different from what the Hmong had known, they might as well have been dropped on the moon.

The greatest problem is language—not just English, but their own as well. Until very recently, Hmong was only a spoken language and, therefore, did not have its own alphabet. Almost none of the refugees could read or write. Being illiterate in their own language made learning a new one doubly hard.

In their homeland their survival never depended on language or the printed word, but on how well they could grow crops and raise livestock. Living on remote mountainsides in small tribes and having little contact with other people, the Hmong did not need their own currency or the kind of rules and regulations Westerners take for granted.

It has been said the Hmong live to work. Yet when they first arrived in America they were crowded into government-owned apartments and were unable to find jobs. This drastic change in lifestyle actually led to the deaths of otherwise healthy Hmong men. This mysterious illness, perhaps caused by extreme culture shock, is called sudden unexplained death syndrome (SUDS).

Still, almost thirty years after the Vietnam War's end and the arrival of the first group of Hmong, there is reason for optimism. Many Hmong children have now graduated from American high schools and colleges and gone on to professional careers. Parents watch with a mixture of fear and delight as their children move into the American mainstream. They are happy the future holds promise for their sons and daughters but are sorry to see them move away from the traditional Hmong culture and customs.

Many wonder if the older Hmong will ever truly become Americans or if they are just waiting for the day the Communist government in Laos will collapse and they can return to their mountain homes. Yand Dao, who became the first Hmong to receive a Ph.D. from an American university, is philosophical: "It is only here, in the United States that the Hmong are able to learn that the young can go to school and become important members of a society. Even if we some day go back to Laos, we will have the tools to play an important part in the action and not have to stick to the mountains."[28]

Tiger Woods

Golfer
1975–

All races and ethnic groups would like to claim Tiger Woods as their own. His career as a golfer has been described in such superlatives as "youngest ever," "first ever," and "greatest ever." The son of an African American father, Earl, many assume Tiger is African American. His mother, however, is from Thailand, and Tiger Woods once told a reporter that he marks "Asian" on forms that ask about racial identity. Yet "Asian" and "African" are only part of his remarkable story. He is, in fact, the first international superstar to proudly proclaim himself multiracial. Where race is concerned, he often says, "Do I have to be either one thing or the other?"

Tiger's given name is Eldrick Woods, but even his parents have never called him that. He was given the nickname Tiger in honor of a South

Vietnamese soldier, Nguyen "Tiger" Phong, who saved Earl's life when he fought as a Green Beret during the Vietnam War. By the time Tiger was born in 1975, Earl and Kultida Woods were settled in California. Out of the military and working regular hours, Mr. Woods finally was able to learn to play the demanding game of golf. He had always been a strong athlete, but mastering golf—an expensive game, once played only by whites—had never been possible.

Not surprisingly, after Tiger's birth Earl Woods found a way to combine his two passions. While the baby watched, Mr. Woods putted in his living room or hit buckets of balls at the driving range. By the time Tiger Woods could walk he was eager to play, too. One day Earl handed Tiger a shortened club and then watched as the toddler lined himself up and took a swing that could only be called "perfect." Earl let out a cry and went to find Kultida. Their son, he shouted, was a golf genius.

Tiger Woods was so good at such a young age that he often made headlines. He won his first competition when he was three; the others boys were ten and eleven. He appeared on television, telling stunned interviewers that he would one day beat the best golfers in the world. By the time he was sixteen he had won the U.S. Junior Amateur Championship.

Despite the distractions of appearing in golf tournaments around the country, Tiger Woods graduated from high school in 1994. That same summer he won the U.S. Amateur Championship and then, in the fall, enrolled at Stanford University. Two years later, after several more amateur titles, including the National Collegiate Championship, Tiger turned professional. By the end of 1996 he was *Sports Illustrated*'s Sportsman of the Year, and fans everywhere were in the grips of "Tigermania."

Since then Tiger Woods has more than met people's huge expectations of him. In 1997 he became the youngest player to win the legendary Masters Tournament, and he won by the largest margin ever. By the end of that year he became the youngest player ever to be ranked the number one professional golfer. When, in 2001, he won the Masters again, he became the first player in history to win all four major tournaments—the Masters, the PGA, the British Open, and the U.S. Open—in a row. The list of Tiger's firsts is long and growing longer. As an African American, Asian American, or multiracial superstar—or simply as the world's greatest golfer—his accomplishments fill people everywhere with awe and pride.

Michelle Kwan

Figure Skater
1980–

A person's life is like a house, Danny Kwan liked to tell his children, and you cannot have all the windows open at the same time. His daughter Michelle has chosen to keep two windows open: skating and school. Others—friends, hobbies, parties—may open slightly from time to time but mostly stay shut tight.

When she is at school, Michelle Kwan insists she is "all school." And when she is on the ice, she is only a skater. But, of course, not just *any* skater. Michelle Kwan has been called one of the greatest champions of all time. She has won four World Championships, five national titles, the silver medal in the 1998 Olympics, and the bronze medal in 2002. The words used to describe her skating range from "elegant" to "sophisticated" to "heavenly."

She is a strong jumper, as all top skaters must be, but that is never what spectators remember most about her performances. It looks, they often say, as if she skims the ice, just hovering over it. The height of her jumps seems to come not from digging a steel blade into the ice but from a magical power that lifts her into the air.

Michelle Kwan began skating when she was five years old, taking lessons with her older sister, Karen. Both girls showed promise and were soon encouraged to travel each weekend from their home outside Los Angeles to a well-known training rink two hours away at Lake Arrowhead. The cost of skating and the time spent driving were a burden on the Kwan family. Danny, a systems analyst for a telephone company, and his wife Estella often worked nights at the Golden Pheasant, a Chinese restaurant owned by Danny's parents. Yet Danny Kwan told his daughters that he would make the commitment to skating as long as they did, too. "We had no vacations," Karen Kwan once explained to a reporter. "No days off. We skated on Christmas Day."

Success came quickly to both girls. Yet despite Michelle Kwan's climb in the rankings, she wanted to move up even faster. At eleven she was already impatient with the pace of junior competitions and longed to skate as a senior. Her coach, however, saw it differently. Frank Carroll liked his young skaters to stay at the junior level as long as possible, both so they could master the difficult jumps and let the judges get to know them. Michelle did not care; she wanted to move up to the highest level. And so, without telling either Mr. Carroll or her parents, she took and passed the test that allowed her to compete as a senior. She was not yet twelve years old.

Her boldness paid off. Less than two years later, Michelle Kwan was ranked third in the United States, just behind Nancy Kerrigan and Tonya Harding. In January 1994 Nancy Kerrigan was attacked and injured during the U.S. Nationals and was unable to finish that competition. Michelle Kwan finished second behind Tonya, but when Nancy recovered enough to skate on the Olympic team, Michelle Kwan became an alternate. She traveled to Lillehammer, Norway, with the Olympic team but never competed. After watching from the sidelines, she vowed that four years later she would be the one to beat.

The next year, 1995, Michelle Kwan was second in the U.S. Nationals. At the World Championships she skated flawlessly but was only fourth. It was then that some of the older skaters, particularly Nancy Kerrigan, told her it was time for a new look. Michelle Kwan exchanged her ponytail for a bun and took care with her clothes and makeup. The new sophisticated look went perfectly with her long program, called *Salome*, and the very next year Michelle Kwan won her first World Championship.

By 1998, a new young skater named Tara Lipinski had grabbed both the number one ranking and the media's attention. Tara's jumps and spins were thrilling but her artistry could not compare with Michelle's. At the Olympics in Japan, Michelle Kwan won the short program, earning several perfect scores. She was nervous before her long program though, believing that one mistake would cost her the gold medal. When she took the ice, she seemed to think her way through her performance rather than just allow her body do what it had done hundreds of times before. Tara's skating, on the other hand, was passionate and energetic, and the judges rewarded her all-out courage with the gold medal while Michelle received the silver. Tara retired from skating soon after the Olympics. Michelle, who did not want to leave skating with words like "timid" and "cautious" ringing in her ears, vowed to compete once again at the 2002 Olympics. She did and won a bronze medal at Salt Lake City.

Life has changed for Michelle Kwan since 1998. She has added more world and national titles to her long list of skating accomplishments, but she has also moved out of her parent's home and enrolled at the University of

California at Los Angeles. Trying to be a normal college student has helped her cope with the pressure of remaining a top female skater. As soon as she finishes a competition in Europe, Asia, or elsewhere in North America, she returns to Los Angeles, picks up her book bag, pulls a baseball cap down low over her famous face, and heads to the UCLA campus. Switching gears—from triple toe loops to philosophy essays—is a big challenge. And that is exactly what Michelle Kwan likes best.

Anoushka Shankar

Sitar Player
1982–

She made her concert debut at age thirteen and has already performed at Carnegie Hall and accompanied the London Symphony Orchestra. The British Parliament gave her a House of Commons Shield in honor of her artistry and musicianship. She appeared on the album *Chants of India* with the late George Harrison of the Beatles. "Uncle George," as Anoushka Shankar called him, was a dear friend of her father, Ravi Shankar, the renowned Indian classical musician.

Actually, Anoushka Shankar leads a double life. When she is not traveling the world in flowing saris playing classical Indian music, she goes home to California, where she wears halter tops, listens to hard rock, and enjoys an occasional trip to the mall. Growing up near San Diego, she happily spent the days with her school friends but returned home to her family's "Indian music room." There her mother taught her to sing and her father, the man credited with introducing classical Indian music to the West, taught her to play the sitar.

Ravi Shankar needed coaxing before he would teach his youngest daughter the sitar. Not only is it very unusual for a girl or woman to play the long-necked Indian lute, but Ravi Shankar's own musical instruction had been carried out in the traditional Indian way. In this highly disciplined approach, a pupil comes to understand that he is called, or chosen by God, to learn a certain instrument. Only then does the pupil seek out a guru, or spiritual guide, with whom he lives for at least seven years. Would Anoushka, born in London and raised in southern California, have the will to learn? Perhaps, but Ravi Shankar wanted more evidence of her inner conviction.

Anoushka's mother, Sukanya, saw it differently. She and her daughter had sung traditional Indian songs since Anoushka was three. Sukanya believed her daughter was ready to learn the sitar and simply needed guidance to accept the sacrifices of learning such a difficult instrument. When Ravi Shankar finally agreed to teach his nine-year-old daughter, he crafted a baby sitar for her. Anoushka Shankar was surprised at the extreme technical difficulty of playing this instrument. She struggled at first but soon began to enjoy the time spent learning from and playing with her father.

For his part, Ravi Shankar was truly impressed with his daughter's natural talent. Her inner drive to excel reminded him of his own. Not yet a teenager, Anoushka began appearing with him in concert. At first she assisted him on stage, but then Ravi Shankar decided to split his concerts, allowing her to perform alone during the first half.

Not surprisingly, Anoushka Shankar's swift rise in the music world and her high-profile concert tours provoked some jealousy. Both critics and other musicians sometimes wondered if she would have gone so far, so fast, if she had not had the name Shankar. She is now used to such talk and knows it will be with her all her life. She believes that people may listen to her the first time because of her father's name, but they will listen the second time because of her own playing.

Today Anoushka Shankar does not question her calling. She proudly states that her second CD, called *Anourag,* a Hindi word meaning "love and affection," is much more accomplished than her first. Her third CD is called *Live at Carnegie Hall.* On her first solo tour of India, which was a real test of her playing ability, she played improvisationally—making up the music as she played it—and also conducted a New Delhi orchestra. At this point in Anoushka Shankar's young life, nearly all the pieces she has recorded have been written for her by her father. "She inspires me and brings out the best," Ravi Shankar told an interviewer. He sees each of his compositions as a blessing which he gives to his daughter and which she then returns many times over.

Notes

1. Davida Malo. *Hawaiian Antiquities* (Moolelo, Hawaii). Honolulu, Hawaii, 1898, p. xii.

2. Edmund H. Worthy Jr. "Yung Wing in America." *Pacific Historical Review* XXXIV, no. 4, 1965, pp. 265–87.

3. Ibid., p. 272.

4. Betty Lee Sung. *Mountain of Gold: The Story of the Chinese in America.* New York: Macmillan, 1967, p. 24.

5. Ibid., p. 195.

6. L.C. Tsung. "The Marginal Man" (reprinted in *The Chinese Americans* by Milton Meltzer. New York: Thomas Y. Crowel, 1980).

7. Rhyme, Sung, p. 24.

8. Deborah Gesensway and Mindy Roseman. *Beyond Words: Images from America's Concentration Camps.* Ithaca, NY: Cornell University Press, 1987, pp. 18–19.

9. Ibid., p. 56.

10. *Current Biography,* "James Wong Howe." New York: H.W. Wilson, 1943, p. 315.

11. Isamu Noguchi. Application for Guggenheim in 1926: "Desire to view nature . . ."

12. Craig Sharlin and Lilia V. Villanueva. *Philip Vera Cruz: A Personal History of Filipino Immigrants and the Farm Workers Movement.* Los Angles: UCLA Labor Center, Institute of Industrial Relations and UCLA Asian American Studies Center, 1992, p. 146.

13. Carlos Bulosan. *America Is in the Heart.* Seattle: University of Washington Press, 1973, p. 236.

14. An Wang. *Lessons: An Autobiography.* Reading, MA.: Addison-Wesley, 1986, p. 12.

15. *Something about the Author,* Vol. 53, p. 155 [Yoshiko Uchida]. Detroit: Gale Group, 1988.

16. Ibid.

17. *Horn Book,* 12/51, p. 440.

18. *Time* magazine, 12/2/91, p. 69.

19. Leonard S. Marcus. "Rearrangement of Memory: An Interview with Allen Say." *Horn Book,* April 30, 1989, p. 28.

20. *Something About the Author,* vol. 53, pp. 91–92.

21. Ibid., p. 92.

22. Commission on Wartime Relocations and Internment of Civilians. "Personal Justice Denied." Washington, DC: Government Printing Offices, 1982, p. 18.

23. Janet Nomura Morey and Wendy Dunn. *Famous Asian Americans.* New York: Dutton/Cobblehill Books, 1992, pp. 126–27.

24. *The New Yorker,* 5/1/91, p. 41.

25. *Boston Globe.* "Gish Jen Writes From Two Worlds." March 27, 1991.

26. Gish Jen. *Typical American.* Boston: Houghton Mifflin, 1991, p. 62.

27. Robert K. Schwarz. "Glissando." *New York Times Magazine,* March 24, 1991, p. 32.

28. Spencer Sherman. "The Hmong in America." *National Geographic,* October 1988, pp. 586–610.

For Further Reading

Cao, Lan, and Novas, Himilee. *Everything You Need to Know about Asian American History.* New York: Penguin Books, 1996.

Chan, Sucheng. *Asian Americans: An Interpretive History.* New York: Twayne Publishers, 1991.

————, ed. *Hmong Means Free: Life in Laos and America.* Philadelphia: Temple University Press, 1994.

Chang, Leslie. *Beyond the Narrow Gate: The Journey of Four Chinese Women from the Middle Kingdom to Middle America.* New York: Lume, 1999.

Daley, William. *The Chinese Americans.* New York: Chelsea House Publishers, 1996.

Dinnerstein, Leonard, and Reimers, David M., eds. *Ethnic Americans: A History of Immigration.* New York: Columbia University, 1999.

Hong, Maria, ed. *Growing Up Asian American*. New York: Avon Books, 1993.

Kim, Elaine H., and Yu, Eui-Young. *East to America: Korean American Life Stories*. New York: The New Press, 1996.

Kim, Elizabeth. *Ten Thousand Sorrows: The Extraordinary Journey of a Korean War Orphan*. New York: Doubleday, 1992.

Kim, Hyung-Chan, ed. *Dictionary of Asian American History*. New York: Greenwood Press, 1986.

Kitano, Harry. *The Japanese Americans*. New York: Chelsea House Publishers, 1996.

Lee, Joann. *Asian Americans: Oral Histories of First to Fourth Generation Americans from China, the Philippines, Japan, India, the Pacific Islands, Vietnam, and Cambodia*. New York: The New Press, 1992.

Ling, Huping. *Surviving on the Gold Mountain: A History of Chinese American Women and Their Lives*. Albany: State University of New York Press, 1998.

Okihiro, Gary. *Margin and Mainstreams: Asians in American History and Culture*. Seattle: University of Washington Press, 1994.

Porte, Barbara Ann. *Hearsay: Strange Tales from the Middle Kingdom*. New York: Greenwillow Books, 1998.

Pran, Dith, ed. *Children of Cambodia's Killing Fields: Memoirs by Survivors*. New Haven: Yale University Press, 1997.

Rutledge, Paul James. *The Vietnamese Experience in America*. Bloomington: Indiana University Press, 1992.

Takaki, Ronald. *A Larger Memory: A History of Our Diversity, with Voices*. Boston: Little, Brown & Co., 1998.

————. *Strangers from a Different Shore: A History of Asian Americans*. New York: Penguin Books, 1989.

Index

Numbers in *italics* represent illustrations.

Photo Credits

Photographs © 2003: AP/Wide World Photos: 169 (Eric Risberg), 47, 97, 118, 124, 131, 152, 189; Bancroft Library, University of California, Berkeley: 55, 121; Bishop Museum Archives: 53; Bob Breidenback: 89; Columbia University: 130; Corbis Images: 104 (AFP), cover bottom left, back cover bottom center, 43, 64, 77, 80, 83, 101, 106, 223 (Bettmann), back cover bottom right, 207 (Anthony P. Bolante/Reuters), 220 (Rufus F. Folkks), 256 (Owen Franken), cover top right, 204 (Mitchell Gerber), cover top left, 259 (David Maxwell/AFP), 162 (Badzic Milenko/AFP), cover bottom center, 244 (Michael Probst/Reuters NewMedia Inc.), 180 (Seattle Post-Intelligencer Collection/Museum of History & Industry), back cover top left, 202, 238 (Mike Segar/Reuters), 159 (Brian Snyder/Reuters), 214 (Susumu Takahashi/Reuters), 262 (Chris Trotman/Duomo), 39 (Underwood & Underwood), 50, 175, 253 (UPI), back cover bottom left, 24, 127, 191; Corbis Sygma: 155 (Stephane Cardinale), 247 (Rick Maiman); Craig Scharlin: 74; Denver Public Library, Western History Collection: 35; Eric Saund: 67; Freedom Forum/Newseum: 136; Getty Images: back cover top center, 133 (Tim Boxer), 194 (George De Sota), 211 (Diane Freed/Newsmakers), 266 (Aundry Gan/Reuters), 149, 172, 182 (Liaison), cover top center, back cover top right, 235 (Newsmakers), cover bottom right, 3, 217 (Mark Wilson); Hulton|Archive/Getty Images: 17, 29, 58, 142; Idaho State Historical Society: 31; Joyce Chen Products: 111; Courtesy of June Kuramoto: 199; Courtesy of Lawrence Yep: 197; Movie Still Archives: 98;

About the Author

Susan Sinnott began her publishing career as an editor for *Cricket*, a literary magazine for children. She later worked at the University of Wisconsin Press, where she managed and edited academic journals. Eventually her own two children pulled her away from scholarly publishing and helped her rediscover the joys of reading and writing books for young people. Ms. Sinnott has written *Zebulon Pike, Jacques Cousteau,* and *Extraordinary Hispanic Americans,* among others, for Children's Press; and *Chinese Railroad Workers, Doing Our Part,* and *Our Burden of Shame: Japanese Internment During World War II* for Franklin Watts. She lives in Eliot, Maine, with her husband and two children.